A MOMENT IN THE MOONLIGHT

KAY CORRELL

Published by Rose Quartz Press

091019

This book is dedicated to Nora. I never met you, but my grandmother called me by your name often.

Find more information on all my books at
kaycorrell.com

COMFORT CROSSING ~ THE SERIES
The Shop on Main - Book One
The Memory Box - Book Two
The Christmas Cottage - A Holiday Novella
(Book 2.5)
The Letter - Book Three
The Christmas Scarf - A Holiday Novella
(Book 3.5)
The Magnolia Cafe - Book Four
The Unexpected Wedding - Book Five

The Wedding in the Grove - (a crossover short

story between series - with Josephine and Paul from The Letter.)

LIGHTHOUSE POINT ~ THE SERIES
Wish Upon a Shell - Book One ✓
Wedding on the Beach - Book Two
Love at the Lighthouse - Book Three
Cottage near the Point - Book Four
Return to the Island - Book Five
Bungalow by the Bay - Book Six

SWEET RIVER ~ THE SERIES
A Dream to Believe in - Book One ✓
A Memory to Cherish - Book Two ✓
A Song to Remember - Book Three ✓
A Time to Forgive - Book Four ✓
A Summer of Secrets - Book Five ✓
A Moment in the Moonlight - Book Six ✓

INDIGO BAY ~ Save by getting Kay's complete collection of stories previously published separately in the multi-author Indigo Bay series. The three stories are all interconnected.
Sweet Days by the Bay

Or buy them separately:

CHAPTER 1

Nora Cassidy wandered along the narrow trail that threaded beside Sweet River, watching and listening to the musical gurgling and splashing as the water slipped over the tumbled rocks. She loved autumn in Sweet River Falls. The aspens turned delectable shades of orange and yellow, and the rustle of their leaves wove an enchanting melody around her. The air held a crisp, clean, refreshing quality. She sucked in a long, deep breath, filling her lungs with the vibrant air.

She loved this daily walk from her cabin to the main building at the lodge. Her time to regroup, recharge, and run through her plans for the day. She had a busy schedule, as usual. There was a wedding this weekend at the new chalet they'd finished this summer. The Stuart sisters had that mostly under control, though.

She smiled when she thought of them as the Stuart sisters. They'd both recently gotten married. Her son, Jason, had married Bree, and Cece had married Zach Berry. They'd had a beautiful double wedding just a few weeks ago. But they'd always be the Stuart sisters in her mind.

She turned at the point where the trail veered away from the river and headed toward Lone Elk Lake. As she neared the lake, a great blue heron sat on a small outcropping of rocks. A blue heron, her late husband's favorite bird. She smiled and waved to him.

"Hi, Ronnie. What you been up to?"

The majestic bird stared at her.

"I miss you, you know. Every single day."

The heron gave her one more look as if he were checking up on her and telling her to have a good day, then spread his large wings and took off, soaring above the lake.

Yes, it was going to be a great day. But she thought that every morning. Who could want more from life than all the blessings she'd been given? Running the inn with her son. Her two children happily married. And she had two healthy grandsons. *And* her best friend, Annie, had married the love of her life. Yes, things were going very well these days. Very well.

Okay… except for the whole rezoning of Lone Elk Lake. *That* was going to be a disaster if she didn't find some way to stop it.

THINGS COULDN'T GET MORE SCREWED up if Harrison Stanworth tried. He did *not* have time to go gallivanting across the country, but he knew it was the right thing to do. He had responsibilities too numerous to count, but his mother would always get his top billing.

"So, you'll go to Sweet River Falls and check out what's going on? I'd be so sad to see the property leave our family's hands. Generations of the Dobbs family have owned the land. I would miss going there if it's sold. I'd go check it out myself but my silly doctor has refused to let me fly." A frown creased his mother's wrinkled face, though her eyes were sharp and crystal clear. "He treats me like an old woman."

"You're not an old woman and, I can go for you." He tried to sound enthusiastic, but he'd already started a mental list of all the things he'd have to cancel in the next week.

"I appreciate you doing this. I do know that your cousin, Walter, wants to sell the property. He sent me the paperwork. It seems like a fair price for the place, doesn't it?" His mother took a sip of tea from a dainty, floral teacup.

No, it didn't. But he wasn't going to say that to her now. He needed to do some more research.

"I still can't imagine some other family owning the land. I just can't. But you and Walter are the last of the family left. Well, except for me. Without another descendant of Jeremiah Dobbs to inherit it, since neither you nor Walter have children, I know someone else will own it eventually… but I didn't think it would be so soon."

No, he didn't have children. He'd been too busy with his career to invest time into any relationship when he was younger. Then he'd just gotten comfortable being a bachelor.

And as far as he was concerned, Walt had done the world a great service in not procreating and passing on *his* genes. The world didn't need another Walter Dobbs.

Okay, that was a nasty thought, but his

cousin was nowhere on his list of people he liked. Walt was more on the top of the list of people he distrusted with a strong dislike that *almost* bordered on hatred.

He leaned over and kissed his mother's cheek. "I'll wrap things up here and try to get a flight out tomorrow."

"Thank you, dear." She smiled. A weaker smile than usual. Her usual bright, perky self had dimmed a bit. He supposed that was expected at seventy-plus years old. Not that she'd ever admit how many years over seventy. But he'd always assumed his trim, athletic mother would outlive him.

That is until this last summer when she'd slowed down significantly. She'd given up a seniors' exercise class that she'd done for years with the same group of women. He couldn't imagine a room of seventy-something women doing their exercises, but it had made her happy and kept her moving. She'd even been an avid tennis player up until a few years ago.

But he'd do anything for her. It had just been him and his mother for years now. His father had died over twenty years ago.

He had to admit he was curious about how the town and their cabin and property would be now. He remembered it as a sleepy little Colorado town. His grandparents' cabin was right on the edge of Lone Elk Lake. It was an ever-growing cabin where each generation had added on until the rambling additions had taken on a twisted, though charming, quality.

His cousin Walt lived in the cabin now. Had for years. Not that it mattered. There were no other family members who wanted to live there.

He pulled himself away from his thoughts. "I'd better go."

"I really appreciate you doing this for me. I'm not quite up to the travel yet. This silly virus that hit me this summer, then the pneumonia. I'm not used to feeling so... unhealthy and not fit." A determined look crossed her face. "But I'll get over this. Just need a bit more time."

"I'm sure you will, Mom." He was sure. Mostly. He'd seen his mother do anything and everything she put her mind to. No reason to think this time would be any different.

CHAPTER 2

The next day Nora drove down Main Street looking for a place to park near Bookish Cafe. She'd promised Annie that she'd drop by for coffee and a chat. They both were busy running their businesses but tried to make time at least once a week to meet and catch up.

It was her lucky day. An empty spot right in front of the shop. She slowed down and flicked on her turn signal.

Before she could pull into the spot, a flashy black sports car whipped into the space, and she had to throw on her brakes to keep from slamming into it. She instinctively hit the horn. The man barely glanced at her as he finished maneuvering into the spot.

Okay, then.

Tourists.

A blessing and a curse.

She continued down the street, not finding a single spot, then circled around a second time until she found another space and pulled into it. She slid out of the car and hurried down the sidewalk toward Annie's shop.

The door swung open as she reached for it, and a tall, dark-haired man stepped through the door, juggling a cup of coffee while texting on his phone and paying no attention to where he was going.

He ran into her, and she bumped against his hard chest with a thud. His phone and the cup he was carrying went flying, spraying her with drops of coffee.

"Oof." The man reached out to steady her with a glare plastered on his clean-shaven, chiseled face. "You should watch where you're going." He reached down and snatched up his phone, checking it carefully.

"*I* should watch where I'm going? You're the one walking out messing with your phone and not paying attention."

He glanced at his phone again. "I... was working."

Like that was an excuse? She brushed at the

now-stained jacket and shirt she was wearing. Picked a bad day to wear a white shirt.

He was probably one of those people who texted and drove too. She waited for him to say he was sorry.

He just stood there staring at her.

She moved sideways to get around him to go inside, annoyed and more flustered than she should be at the run-in.

He reached out and caught her arm. "Sorry 'bout that."

She glanced at his face and didn't really think it said anything about truly being sorry. His bright blue eyes stared at her a moment longer, then he turned and walked over to the black sports car that had cut her off. It chirped as he pushed the button on the remote, and he swung open the door.

Of course, he was the rude space-grabbing tourist.

She turned her back on him, leaned down to pick up the cup he'd left sitting on the sidewalk, and slipped into the shop, the piercing look in his eyes still etched into her mind.

Annie walked up to her. "What happened to you?" She pointed at the stained jacket and shirt.

"I ran into one of your customers… or to be more exact, *he* ran into *me*." Even if the man thought it was the other way around.

"That guy who just left? Tall, handsome? Dark hair and the most intriguing blue eyes?"

Nora scowled. "You're a married woman. What are you doing noticing those things?"

"I try and remember new customers, so I'll recognize them when they come back. Large coffee, black." Annie shrugged.

"Well, he's not going to know how great your coffee is, because it's spilled all over the sidewalk right now."

"Come on. Let's get you cleaned up. Come to my office, then we'll get some coffee and go up to the loft area to chat." Annie turned to Lindsey working at the counter. "I'm taking a break, but call me if you need me."

"Sure thing." Lindsey turned to wait on a new customer.

Nora followed Annie to her office and dabbed ineffectually at the stains. "I'll just work on them when I get back to the lodge and throw them in the wash."

They headed upstairs with their coffee and settled into comfortable chairs overlooking the Sweet River flowing outside the large picture window. She ignored the stains on her clothing and ignored the flashes of the rude tourist's face that flitted through her mind. Annie was right, though, the man did have intriguing eyes.

HARRISON SAT in his rental car, flustered. He wanted another cup of coffee, but he didn't want to go back inside that cafe and run into the same woman again. Either figuratively or literally.

He should have been paying attention when he walked out the door. And he should have apologized appropriately. His mother would be aghast at him right now. But that woman... he'd been so startled when he looked at her.

She looked to be about his age, but who knew with women? She had chestnut brown hair with grey streaked through it and didn't appear to be the type of woman who worried about that. And her eyes. Those were what captured his attention. They were amber with flecks of deep brown.

And they'd flashed with annoyance.

He couldn't blame her. He'd run into her, acted like a jerk, then escaped to his car.

And he'd left his spilled paper coffee cup sitting there on the sidewalk. And he never littered. Ever.

He'd spied her leaning down and picking up his mess.

Now he was paying the price. He'd only had a lousy airline cup of coffee on his early flight, and now, the coveted coffee he'd been craving all day was poured over the sidewalk.

He turned on the car and pulled away. Feeling sheepish, he went in search of another cup of coffee. Anywhere but Bookish Cafe where the woman he'd run into was probably ranting about him and his loutish behavior.

He glanced at the battered file resting on the seat beside him. He'd gone over the printouts and taken notes on the flight. He had so many questions, and he was pretty certain this was not a fair deal. At least not a fair deal for his mother.

Coffee, then a bit of research on what's been going on with the town since he left. And he had to find a place to stay, too. He didn't want Walt to know he was in town. Not just yet.

CHAPTER 3

Later that afternoon, Nora stood behind the reception desk at the lodge checking in a Linda Seabridge from Baltimore. The woman looked to be in her early to mid-forties and in good physical shape. Not surprising, the area attracted quite a crowd of people wanting to explore the numerous trails around Sweet River Falls.

"What brings you to Sweet River Falls?" Nora asked as she handed back the woman's card.

"I..." The woman paused and looked confused. "I... um, just heard about the area. Thought I'd come check it out. It's very lovely here."

"We think so. Let me know if you need any recommendations for hiking trails or places to visit while you're here."

"I will." The woman smiled.

Nora handed her a key. "I've put you in Serenity Cabin. You'll have a nice view of the lake."

"Thank you."

"You can park right in front of it. Here's a map to get to it, but just go to the left when you leave here and you'll find it."

Nora watched as the woman walked out of the reception area. She turned around to the counter behind her and started working on some paperwork. Always paperwork.

"Ah, hem. Excuse me."

She'd been so engrossed in her papers, she'd neglected the front desk. She turned at the sound.

"You."

"You."

There he stood. *Him*. The man from her run-in in town.

He recovered first. "I… I'm looking for a place to stay. Probably a week or so."

As much as she wanted to say they were full,

they weren't. Those blue eyes stared at her, and she did her best to ignore them.

Intriguing eyes.

Nope.

Ignorable eyes.

"We do have an available cabin for you."

"Great."

She didn't really know if she thought it was great that this rude man was going to be here for a week or so… and he better not litter on the property either.

"Name?"

He paused. "Harrison. Harrison Stanworth."

She checked him in. Mistyping Chicago and *street* of all things as she entered his information. "Here you go." She handed him the key to Rustic Haven.

He stared down at the key in his hand. "No door card?"

"Nope, just a good old-fashioned key. You know how to work one, right?" She cocked her head to one side.

He rewarded her with a lazy grin. "I do."

He closed his fist around the key. "And… uh… I just wanted to apologize properly for…

for earlier. I'm sorry. I wasn't watching where I was going."

Ah, ha! Vindication swept through her. "No problem."

"I see you've changed into less... splattered clothes."

She looked down at the old blue plaid shirt that she'd rapidly tossed on after changing out of her stained clothes. She wished she'd taken the time to put on something a little bit nicer.

But that was *silly*. She often wore flannel shirts here at the lodge. They were practical. And if someone was going to throw coffee on her, it wouldn't show as much...

She ignored his discussion of her apparel. "Here's a map to the cabin. It's called Rustic Haven, but actually, it's been recently remodeled. There's dinner here at the lodge starting in about an hour."

"Thank you. Not sure of my dinner plans yet." He looked at his watch. "Wi-fi in the cabin?"

"Yes. You should get a fairly decent signal. Usually. If not, you can come to the main lodge. We get the best signal here."

He nodded.

"Let me know if you need anything."

"I will." He turned away, and she watched him cross the floor with long, confident strides. His whole demeanor reflected the fact that he was a man used to getting his way.

But he *had* apologized, there was that.

LINDA SLOWLY UNPACKED her things at Serenity Cabin. Serenity. She wasn't sure she'd ever feel serene again. Not after what she'd recently found out.

Her life had been upended, and she'd struggled to find her footing ever since.

So many lies.

So many surprises.

She didn't really know what to do. But one thing was sure. She was going to find out the truth.

An ache filled her chest with a pain so raw it made her knees go weak. She sank onto the colorful quilt on the bed and lowered her head into her hands.

She sat there for long minutes, waiting for the ache to subside, waiting for the strength to stand and finish unpacking. She had plans for her stay in Sweet River Falls, and she needed to get started on them.

But still, she sat.

HARRISON SORTED through the papers he'd placed on the table in his cabin. Other real estate deals in the area. Land prices. Housing market info. No matter how he looked at the deal Walt had sent to his mother, it just didn't seem like a good price for the land and cabin. It was prime lakefront property.

And for the life of him, he couldn't believe that Walt wasn't sharp enough to get top dollar for the property.

He looked at the offer again and all the paperwork Walt had sent to his mother to sign. Did Walt think that his mother was a doddering old fool who would sign anything? Did Walt think that he wouldn't look after his own mother on this deal?

Well, he knew what his cousin thought about him. Walt thought he was some stupid loser.

Well, his cousin had a surprise coming. He wasn't the same person Walt had last seen what seemed like a life time ago.

He set the paper down on the table and rubbed his eyes. The room had grown dark while he worked. He glanced at his watch as his stomach rumbled. He'd fully intended to head into town to eat dinner... if only to avoid running into that woman again. What a weird coincidence that she worked at the very place he'd picked to stay.

But now his hunger was overcoming his decision to avoid *her*. He'd only grabbed a breakfast burrito at the airport and skipped lunch.

It sounded so easy to just walk over to the dining lodge and grab something to eat. With any luck, *she* would still be working the front desk and he could slip into the dining room unnoticed.

He frowned. He didn't even know her name. Only that she worked at the lodge. His sum total of knowledge about her. That, and he knew she had remarkable eyes that still haunted and taunted him.

He grabbed his jacket and walked down to the trail beside the lake. The end of the sunset tossed rays of shimmering gold across the water. He paused, remembering the sunsets when he was a young boy. His mother had loved to watch the sunsets here. How many times had he sat out with her on the large boulder at the water's edge in front of his grandparents' cabin? He stood silently, lost in memories, and watched until the sun finished slipping below the horizon, then he headed toward the lodge.

The dining room bustled with activity, and a man walked up to him, menus in hand. "Hi, table for one?"

"Yes, just me."

"Follow me."

He followed the man to a table on the far side of the dining room. He looked left and right as they walked, glad to see no evidence of the run-in woman. He took his seat and the offered menu.

"You staying here at the lodge?"

"I am."

"Mom said we got a couple more guests this afternoon."

Mom?

His confusion must have been evident.

"My mother. Nora Cassidy. She and I own the lodge." The man stretched out a hand. "I'm Jason Cassidy."

"Nice to meet you." He said the words automatically, still processing the information.

Nora Cassidy. The run-in woman had a name. And she *owned* the lodge.

"I'll send your waitress right over."

He nodded and opened the menu, not really reading the words. It was probably going to be really hard to avoid the woman—Nora—if she owned the lodge where he was staying…

CHAPTER 4

Nora served the customers in the dining room the next morning, looking up every now and then to see if that Harrison Stanworth fellow was going to come in for breakfast. Jason had said he'd been in for dinner last night, but she'd been busy in the kitchen helping Judy with the cooking.

She smiled at—what was her name? Linda something. The woman from Baltimore who had checked in yesterday afternoon. "More coffee?"

"Yes, please."

Nora filled Linda's cup. "You have plans for the day?"

"I thought I might go into town. I wanted to visit the town's historical society."

"Good day for that. It's only open three days a week, but today is one of them." Nora paused. "Any particular history you're interested in? I grew up here. Know a lot about the area."

Linda's eyes lit up. "You did?"

"Yep, born and raised here. Raised my kids here, too."

"So you know most of the people who own property on the lake?"

"Most of them, why? You looking for lake property?" A waitress came by and took the coffee pot from Nora and walked over to an adjacent table to refill another customer's cup. All her employees knew that she liked to take time to chat with the guests and get to know them. So many of them came back as repeat guests and became almost like family.

"No, I... no. Not looking for property. I just..." Linda looked down at the coffee and traced a finger along the edge of the mug. "No, I'm just interested in... history."

"Ah, a history buff." Nora smiled.

Linda nodded, but Nora got the feeling it wasn't really a nod of total agreement, more of a nod of don't-ask-more-questions. Okay, she wasn't here to pry into her guests' lives.

"Well, I hope you enjoy yourself. There are

copies of old newspapers—not many have been scanned in yet, but they are working on it. Some books about the early people in the town. Lots of photographs. Eleanor is the historian there. I'm sure she'll be able to help you."

"Thank you."

"Sure thing. Let me know if you need anything else."

Nora walked away, a frown tugging the corners of her mouth. There was something about Linda, but she couldn't quite put her finger on what was bothering her about the woman.

HARRISON WAS HOPING his luck from last night would hold and he wouldn't run into Nora at the dining room this morning. He was starving, and he'd seen the menu for breakfast in his cabin. Probably set there to entice the guests. And entice it did. He rarely had time for breakfast at home, but either the mountain air or *something* made him ravenous here in Sweet River Falls.

A woman with brown, shoulder-length hair passed him as he entered the lodge. Her sky-blue eyes searched his face quickly as she walked past. He frowned and turned to watch her leave. Something about her… He didn't know her. At least he didn't think he did. But something about her seemed so… familiar.

He shrugged away the thought and concentrated on the wonderful aroma that swirled around him. Maple. Cinnamon. Fresh baked bread.

He strode across the last of the distance in anticipation, entered the dining room, and froze.

She was here. Nora Cassidy.

She looked up, and he knew she saw him standing there. Electricity crackled between them. No way to deny it. No time to change his mind and head into town for breakfast.

He plastered on a weak smile. The woman made him feel foolish and awkward, and those weren't emotions he was used to feeling. She motioned him to cross the room, and he did as he was beckoned.

"Good morning." Nora smiled at him, but the smile was that of someone who was used to greeting her guests, not a smile that said she was truly glad to see him.

And why would she be glad to see him?

He'd run into her, ruined her clothes, and then hadn't apologized. Well, he'd apologized yesterday afternoon, but even he knew that was too little, too late.

"Good morning." He slipped into the chair at the table she motioned to. "Lovely day here." *Lovely* day? What kind of greeting was that? That didn't even sound like him. She threw him off balance, and he didn't like that one bit.

"Supposed to get a long string of wonderful autumn weather. You should go hike some trails —if you're into that kind of thing—the aspens are glorious this time of year."

"I might just do that." But he'd have to find some hiking boots and something to wear. He hadn't really packed appropriately, he realized. He'd just been thinking about doing some research, meeting some people, getting some facts and figures. He hadn't thought about actually getting out and enjoying the beautiful scenery while he was here. He'd forgotten just how breath-taking the views were.

He looked down at his precisely creased slacks and light blue, button-down shirt. Not really lodge and hiking apparel.

"Say, do you know where I could go and get some other clothes?" He unbuttoned his cuffs and rolled up his sleeves, striving to do so nonchalantly.

"Sure do. Alpine Outfitters. Tell Chuck I sent you. Chuck Smith. I'm Nora Cassidy by the way."

"Nice to properly meet you, Nora."

She gave him a small smile. "A better meeting than our first one."

"I am sorry. I apologize again."

"It wasn't a big deal." Nora started to turn away. "I'll send your waitress over. I'd suggest the pecan pancakes. Judy makes fabulous pecan pancakes."

He watched her walk away and disappear through the doorway to the kitchen. He frowned and turned his attention back to her remark about Alpine Outfitters.

Chuck Smith. It couldn't be the *same* Chuck Smith, could it? Not the one he'd known as a kid when he'd come to visit his grandparents?

NORA PUTTERED AROUND THE KITCHEN, letting the two servers deal with the customers.

"You look a little flushed." Judy, the cook,

took another batch of cinnamon rolls from the oven and set them on the counter.

"I do?"

"You do."

Well, that annoyed her. She wasn't overheated in the least bit, but she could feel a slight flush to her cheeks. She wanted to blame it on the oven that was just opened, but she knew the truth.

Harrison.

He'd unnerved her again when he'd looked at her with those sparkling clear eyes of his. Eyes that seemed to look right inside of her. She shivered.

"You coming down with something?" Judy frowned.

"No, I'm fine." Or she would be if she could just avoid Harrison. Or at least find a way for him to not get under her skin.

It had been a long time—a very long time—since a man had affected her like this. And she was pretty certain she didn't like it. Not one bit.

CHAPTER 5

Harrison returned to his cabin after breakfast without seeing Nora again. He wasn't sure if that was a good thing or a bad thing.

He sat at the table and started doing more research on his laptop. After a while, he closed the computer and decided to take a break. He drove into town and passed by Alpine Outfitters. He did want to get some more appropriate clothes but really didn't want to run into Chuck Smith. *If* the owner Chuck was the same Chuck he'd known. And *if* Chuck recognized him. It had been over forty years. But he'd have to give his credit card with his name on it. And Chuck would recognize his name. *If* it was *that Chuck.*

He frowned. And if Chuck was still friends

with Walt, then he might mention to Walt that he was in town. With a split-second decision, he decided to drive over to the neighboring town of Mountain Grove and see what stores they had there. Surely he could get what he needed there.

He drove the short distance to Mountain Grove, marveling at the scenery as the roadway threaded its way around mountains and dipped down into the large valley between the two towns. He found a store in Mountain Grove and twenty minutes of shopping later, came out with flannel shirts, a couple pairs of jeans, and a pair of shoes that seemed to be a hybrid of hiking boots and tennis shoes. He'd been tempted to buy a cowboy hat because he'd always wanted one when he'd come to Colorado to visit. But he'd been too much of a dork then to pull it off. He still didn't think he could pull it off now without looking ridiculous.

And once again he was ravenous. He'd spied a tavern on the edge of town, Mac's Place, and decided to go grab some lunch there. He really was going to have to go on some hikes while he was here, if for no other reason than to burn off all the calories he was consuming.

He pushed through the door to the tavern

and walked up to sit at the long, wooden bar. The man behind the bar greeted him. "Afternoon." He pushed a menu his direction. "Can I get you something to drink?"

"Iced tea would be great."

"Coming up." The man walked away, and Harrison looked at the menu. A double bacon cheeseburger and fries called his name. So much for his usual healthy eating habits.

The man returned and slid a tall glass of tea to him. "Just passing through?"

"I'm actually staying in Sweet River Falls for a week or so."

"Really? Where?"

"At Sweet River Lodge."

The man grinned. "Great choice. My wife's mother owns it. Nora Cassidy. Have you met her?"

Man, he just could *not* get away from her. He smiled weakly. "Yes, we've met."

"She's great. Wonderful mother-in-law. I'm sure you'll enjoy your stay there." The man extended a hand. "I'm Mac McKenna."

"Harrison." He shook the man's hand.

"What brings you to Mountain Grove?"

It wasn't like he could tell the man why he'd come here... to avoid being recognized.

"Just touring around the area. Seeing the sights."

Mac nodded. "Can I take your order?"

Harrison ordered his definitely-not-on-his-usual-diet meal only feeling *slightly* guilty. Okay, he felt *pretty* guilty, but he ordered it anyway.

Mac soon returned with the lunch, and Harrison eyed it hungrily. "Here you go. Enjoy."

"I'm sure I will."

And he did. Every last bite of it. Almost guilt-free. Almost.

HARRISON PULLED BACK into Sweet River Falls late that afternoon. He spied Bookish Cafe—the scene of his run-in with Nora—and decided to stop in again. He wanted to see if they had some books on the history of the town. Especially any that mentioned his ancestors and the history of the area around Lone Elk Lake. He needed to be totally prepared before he confronted Walt.

He found a parking space and headed into the shop. The same friendly woman who had greeted him yesterday welcomed him.

"Welcome back to Bookish Cafe. Can I help you? Coffee again?"

"No, I'm actually book shopping today. I'm looking for books on the history of the town. Do you have anything like that?"

"Sweet River Falls? We do have a few books over here in the Colorado section." The woman smiled at him. "I'm Annie, by the way. I've lived here my whole life if you have any questions about the area."

"Thanks, Annie. I'm Harrison, and I might just take you up on that offer." First, he'd do more research on his own.

"Are you staying here in Sweet River Falls very long?" Annie made small talk as she led him over to the book section.

"I'm at the Sweet River Falls Lodge for a week or so."

The woman smiled. "Oh, my best friend, Nora, owns the lodge."

Of course Annie was Nora's best friend. He had to keep himself from rolling his eyes. Nora haunted him everywhere he went.

Instead he gave Annie what he now felt was becoming his signature weak smile.

"I'm sure you'll love staying there. It's

beautiful right there on Sweet River and Lone Elk Lake."

"It's very nice." He conveniently left out that he'd grown up spending his summers on the edge of Lone Elk Lake.

"Well, here is the Colorado section. Let me know if you need anything else." Annie left to help another customer.

He started skimming through the books and pulled out a few that caught his attention. He sat down at a nearby chair and started carefully leafing through them, trying to decide which ones would be the most helpful. He looked up when he heard someone approach.

"Oh, sorry. Didn't mean to bother you." The same woman he'd seen leaving the lodge this morning stood before him. "I've been over at the historical society, and Eleanor from there sent me over here with some recommendations of books on the history of the town that they didn't have at the historical society." She nodded at the books in his hands. "I see you're interested in the history, too?"

"I am."

She smiled at him. "Well, don't let me disturb you. I'm just going to browse the shelves a bit."

He frowned as she turned to look at the shelf. It was almost like he knew her or should know her. But he rarely forgot faces, and this one didn't mesh exactly with any memory of anyone he knew. But there was something about her... Her smile reminded him of someone, and her eyes. Still, he couldn't figure it out. It bothered him, but he pushed the puzzle away, letting his subconscious work on it. Maybe it would come to him.

He chose two of the books and went to the counter to check out. The woman who had been browsing came up behind him with her own stack of books.

"Well, it looks like I'm going to have to replenish the books in our Colorado section." Annie smiled at them both.

"You had a great selection. It was hard to decide." The woman set her books on the counter next to his, and he saw she'd gotten one of the same ones he'd decided on.

"Glad I could help you both." Annie reached for his books but turned to the woman. "Are you just passing through? Staying here?"

"I'm in town for... well, I don't know how long. I'm staying at Sweet River Falls Lodge."

"Well, so is Harrison, here. You'll probably

keep running into each other." Annie rung up his books, and he handed her his credit card.

He turned to the woman standing beside him. "I'm Harrison Stanworth." He instantly regretted giving his last name. The fewer people in town who knew his full name, the better for now.

Her eyes widened slightly for the briefest moment. If he hadn't been looking so closely at her, he would have missed it. He swore he saw… something… in her expression. She recovered quickly and said, "I'm Linda Seabridge."

The name didn't ring a bell for him. "Annie's probably right. I guess we'll run into each other. At least if you're eating at the dining room, too."

"I had breakfast there. It was wonderful."

"I did too, and it was," he agreed. He turned and took the offered books. "Thanks for your help, Annie."

"Any time. And come back for coffee."

"I will." He turned to Linda. "I guess I'll see you at the lodge."

"Probably."

He swore he could feel Linda staring at him as he left the shop.

CHAPTER 6

The dining room was crowded this evening. Nora gave Harrison the last open table, a small two-top near the windows. "Here you go." She handed him the menu, and he smiled at her. A warm smile. One that she couldn't reconcile to his rude behavior the first day she'd met him. A smile that made her feel a bit uneasy because it... well, because she didn't *like* the way it made her feel.

Or did she?

And maybe her first impression of him wasn't really how he was. He'd been pleasant ever since and had apologized repeatedly. She just hoped he didn't apologize again...

"What do you suggest tonight?" He opened the menu.

"Can't go wrong with Judy's fried chicken, but she also made meatloaf and mashed potatoes. Great comfort food." She glanced around, looking for his waitress, but she must be in the kitchen. Just then Linda-from-Baltimore came into the dining room, looking a bit overwhelmed that they were so full.

"Say, do you mind sharing your table with another guest? We're full tonight, and she just walked in."

Harrison looked toward the doorway and paused.

"You don't have to say yes if you'd prefer to dine alone."

He nodded. "No, that's fine. Ask her if she'd like to join me. I actually met her at Annie's bookstore. We were both interested in similar books."

Nora walked over to Linda. "We're kind of full tonight, but Harrison, one of our guests, said you could join him at his table. He just sat down. Do you want to join him?"

Linda paused and glanced over to where Harrison sat by the window. "You sure he doesn't mind?"

"Not at all. He said to come ask you."

She smiled. "Okay, then. I'd enjoy having some company for the meal."

Nora led her over to the table, and Linda slipped into the seat across from Harrison. "May I get you two some drinks? Then I'll go find your waitress. We're pretty busy for a Thursday night."

"I'd like the house red wine." Harrison looked at her with his bright blue eyes and slight smile, and a tiny flutter went through her. Which was annoying because she was way too busy and too old for flutters.

She turned to Linda, ignoring Harrison and ignoring his eyes and just ignoring everything about him. "How about you, Linda?"

"I think I'll have tea."

"Okay, I'll get those drinks and find your waitress."

She turned and hurried to the kitchen, annoyed at her reaction to Harrison.

Really annoyed.

"So, have you read any of the books you purchased this afternoon?" Harrison set down his menu, *fully* decided on the meatloaf. Or maybe the fried chicken…

"I just skimmed the first few chapters of one of them." Linda looked down at her menu.

"Nora said the meatloaf and the fried chicken were good choices."

"I think I'll just have a salad." She closed the menu.

Great, go ahead and make healthy eating choices when he was consuming just about anything and everything that was suggested to him. He was going to have to double his time at the gym after this trip. Or maybe he'd put his new purchases to good use and actually go hiking out by the lake.

The waitress—not Nora—brought their drinks, and he was strangely disappointed. They ordered, then sat and sipped their drinks.

"So, why are you so interested in the town's history?" He took a sip of the house wine—it was surprisingly good—and set the glass on the table.

"I—I don't know. I just like to learn about areas I visit, I guess." Linda shrugged. "Like this lake. I was reading about it and some of the original families that settled in the area."

He shot her a look. So she was interested in

the lake area history, too? "So, what did you find out?"

"Not a lot yet. Just some names of early settlers. There was a family with the last name Littleton who settled here. The matriarch of the family was Grace. The book said Grace's Peak was named after her. There was another family that settled here." She paused. "I think their name was Dobbs."

She said it like she was just reciting facts she'd learned, but there was a hint of something in her eyes when she said it.

"So, did *you* find out anything about either of those families?" She looked at him questioningly.

He did not like the way this conversation was headed. The last thing he wanted to do was discuss his family. "Didn't really get time to read them much." Which was an outright lie. He'd devoured every single word he could find about Jeremiah Dobbs, the original buyer of the land, but he sure wasn't going to discuss it with anyone.

"Oh." Disappointment spread across her face, but she quickly hid it with a smile.

Their dinner came, and he changed the topic to safer subjects. Lousy airline food. The

Denver Airport with its remarkable white tent-ish roof. The gorgeous fall weather here. Annie's bookstore. Anything but the lake. And the Dobbs family.

Linda stood after she finished the meal. "Well, thanks for letting me share your table."

"No problem." He watched her walk away and chewed on his bottom lip, still trying to figure out who she reminded him of.

He contemplated ordering a second glass of wine. It really had been exceptionally good—someone knew their wines. He was in no hurry to leave. But why? His finally-decided-on meatloaf dinner was all finished.

He knew why. He was hoping that Nora would drop by his table again. He signaled the waitress and ordered the wine.

CHAPTER 7

"Here, I'll take that to Mr. Stanworth." Nora reached for the glass of wine the waitress was holding. "You go see if that table over there needs anything else. They look like they might be ready for their check." If she'd learned anything in this business, it was to not make people sit and wait for their checks at the end of the meal. A fine dance of not rushing them and not making them wait.

The dining room was clearing out, and the dinner rush was winding down. If they were going to be this busy midweek, she would have to hire more wait staff. She headed over to Harrison's table, knowing full well she could have just as easily checked on the table she'd sent the waitress to.

She approached Harrison's table where he sat staring out the window, lost in thought. "Here you go."

He turned from the window and smiled at her. "Thank you." He reached for the glass. "It's very good wine."

"My daughter-in-law, Bree, really knows her wine. She's a caterer. Anyway, with her help, we've revamped our wine selection recently."

"Looks like most of your customers are leaving..." He paused and looked at her. "Do you think... do you want to join me in a glass of wine?"

She looked around the room, knowing full well that the rest of the staff could wrap things up here but still uncertain if she should join him.

But then, why not?

"You know, that sounds wonderful. I'll go grab myself a glass of that delicious red wine. Wouldn't mind getting off my feet for a bit." She hurried over to the bar area and poured herself a half glass of wine, wondering what she was doing...

She returned to his table and took a seat across from him. She took a sip of the wine. "It's an excellent wine, isn't it? I don't know how

Bree finds such great, reasonably priced wine for us."

"Well, she did a good job with this one."

She wondered how long they could continue talking about the wine…

Harrison set his wine on the table, and she avoided staring at his long fingers wrapped around the glass. He looked directly at her and she took a hurried sip.

He sent her an easy smile. "It was a gorgeous day out today. You're right, the aspen trees are truly beautiful with their leaves changing now. I like how when I walked through the grove of aspens near my cabin, I could hear the whisper of their leaves."

She looked at him in surprise. Not everyone noticed that. The whisper. She loved the enchanting rustle of their leaves too. It was truly magical. "Then I put you in the right cabin because you have to walk through that grove to get to the lake or the dining lodge."

"The cabin is nice. I really like it. Very… cabin-ish, if that's even a term. But nicely decorated, and I noticed the kitchen is well equipped, not that I'll use it. I don't cook."

"Not at all?"

"Well, I heat left-overs from meals I get

when I eat out, if that counts. I usually just pick up takeout, a salad or something, on my way home from work."

"Well then, I hope you at least eat most of your meals here and we can show you what real cooking is like."

He leaned back and patted his stomach. "The food here is delicious. I also had a great lunch at Mac's Place today."

"Oh, my son-in-law owns that."

"Yes, I met him. Nice guy."

"He's a fabulous man. He's a great role model for Beth's sons, too. Their own father is rather... nonexistent... most of the time."

Their conversation lagged, and she took another sip of wine, glancing around the dining room out of habit, making sure everything was being taken care of.

"So you and your son own the lodge?" Harrison was leaning back in his chair, the picture of relaxation.

So why did she feel so tense? She consciously drew in a slow, deep breath and relaxed. "We do. After college he came back here to help me run it."

"Have you owned it long?"

The familiar squeeze to her lungs caused her

to pause. It was still, after all these years, so difficult to talk about. "I have. My husband and I bought it over thirty years ago."

She saw him glance at her left hand where she still wore her simple silver wedding band. "He died just a few years after we bought the place." She twisted the ring with a brush of her thumb. The pain had lessened over the years, of course, but it was still there. Every day. Just hovering below the surface. She'd loved Ronnie with all her heart and had married him believing they'd share their lives and grow old together. But sometimes life had other plans for you.

"I'm sorry." Harrison's eyes brimmed with sympathy. "And you've run it by yourself until Jason joined you?"

"I have."

"That's impressive. It must be a huge job. And the lodge is great." His eyes now shone with admiration.

She shifted in her seat and took another tiny sip of wine, trying to ignore that admiring gaze. "Thank you." She took a cleansing breath and changed the subject. "So, what brings you to Sweet River Falls?"

"I... uh... just taking a little break."

Now his eyes said he was hedging. Maybe he was running away from something. Or taking time to recover from something. Or… Her mind raced with possibilities. She almost laughed at herself. Or maybe he was just taking a vacation like he said. He didn't look like the type of man who took too much time off.

"So what do you do back in Chicago?" Chicago. C-h-i-c-a-g-o. See, she could spell when he wasn't rattling her.

"I work for an investment firm."

"Oh." She didn't really know much about investment firms to carry on a knowledgeable conversation about them. They just… what? Did investments? Bought things?

"I'm in the acquisitions division."

Ah, they did buy things.

"What made you choose Sweet River Falls for your vacation?"

He looked down at his glass, then back up at her. "I like the mountains. Haven't been to them in years. Thought it would be a good place to come and… unwind."

That didn't really answer her question about why he'd chosen *Sweet River Falls*, but she guessed it was close enough. Maybe he'd run across the town's website. Jason had volunteered to work on it, and now they were getting more and more hits on the site. He had a bit of social media going for it, too. The town really needed to hire someone to do that part-time, but ever since Jason had offered to help, they just let him do it for free. She was fairly certain that Dobbs would never suggest putting something in the town's budget to pay Jason for his time...

She brought her thoughts back to Harrison. And his eyes. *No*, not his eyes. She focused on the rich burgundy color of the wine in her glass.

HE FELT BADLY he'd just told Nora a weak half-truth about his visit here to Sweet River Falls. But, really, he didn't want people to know who he was. He still needed to go to county records and see if he could pull the original deed for the property. And last, before Walt found out he was here, he wanted to talk to the law firm that had handled his grandfather's estate. His grandfather's lawyer was long gone, but he had a son working there now.

He took another sip of his wine, wondering how slowly he could sip it and if he could keep

Nora sitting here for as long as it took him to finish it.

"So I read in the brochure in my cabin that you just recently opened a chalet here on the property for weddings and meetings." If he kept her talking about the lodge, she'd sit with him a bit longer, right?

"We did. It turned out wonderful. We're booked almost every weekend now for weddings, and we've had a few small companies book it during the week for meetings."

"Seems like a smart business decision."

"It was. Jason thought of it and dealt with the plans and worked with the builder." Her eyes sparkled when she talked about her son.

"Must be nice to have someone share the workload."

"It is. I don't know what I'd do without him. And his wife, Bree, caters events here. And Bree's sister, Cece, is our wedding planner."

He tried to sort through all the names to keep them straight. "Kind of like one big family." He couldn't imagine having all that family around. For years it had only been his mother and him. Well, Walt had still existed all that time, but Harrison had been determined to pretend he didn't.

She smiled back at him, her warm amber eyes lighting up as she talked about her family and business. "It *is* like one big family, and I wouldn't have it any other way."

"Well, you sure have a beautiful place for the lodge, here on the lake."

"It is. And I hope it stays that way."

He frowned and leaned forward. "What do you mean?"

"Walter Dobbs—he owns a huge chunk of land across the lake—he got zoning approval for selling his land and the right to build a big condo complex. It's going to ruin the whole charm of the lake. And he's trying to get the lake rezoned for motorboats, jet skis, that kind of thing."

He sat back in surprise. This was all news to him. He didn't realize Walt had gotten new zoning regulations approved. And he hadn't known Walt was planning on building *condos*. There was just the simple document about a sale to a trust, and he'd been unable to turn up much on the trust. He thought it might just be someone's family trust, but now he wasn't so sure.

His mother had told him that some new family was buying the cabin and land and hoped they'd love it as much as the Dobbs family had. But it appeared that wasn't exactly Walt's plan. He felt the wrinkles of a frown crease his forehead.

Nora continued. "I've tried everything I can think of to block this. Some people in town would like a big condo complex and the tourists it would bring. But it will give a whole new atmosphere to the lake. I'm sure most of my regulars will quit coming back year after year. They come for the peace and quiet and beauty of the lake. Instead they'll look across to a high-rise condo complex and listen to the drone of motors out on the lake. That will probably mess up the fishing, too."

Walt was always up to some kind of scheme that benefited him, not others. It appeared his cousin hadn't changed one bit over the years, not that it surprised him. He doubled his resolve to dig deeper into this "great deal" Walt had presented to his mother.

"Didn't mean to drop my problems on you." Nora stood. "I should probably go check and see if things are wrapping up in the kitchen."

"No, I didn't mind listening. It does sound like a lot will change in the area if it all happens."

"Oh, it will happen if Dobbs has his way. I just have to figure out a way to stop him." He'd rarely seen a more determined look on anyone's face—not even in heated acquisition negations for his firm. Nora turned and walked away, disappearing into the kitchen. He sat and looked out into the darkness out the window, finishing his wine.

Walt. Always looking out for himself.

He now had no doubt that there was no way this was going to be a fair deal for his mother. His cousin hadn't changed a bit.

LATE THAT EVENING, Nora crossed the well-worn pine-plank floor of her cabin with its familiar squeak in the middle of the room and headed to the mantel over the fireplace. She picked up her favorite picture of Ronnie and traced her finger over his grinning face. With a long sigh, she clasped the photo against her chest. "Oh, Ronnie. I'm trying my best to save this lake. I know you loved it so. I do, too."

She thought back on when they'd first found this ramshackle lodge at the edge of the lake. They'd taken a leap of faith—and all their savings—and put a down payment on the place. Ronnie had worked endlessly updating the cabins, doing repairs, fixing leaking roofs and dripping pipes. Until… one spring he just wore out with any little effort he exerted doing anything. After weeks of chiding him and imploring him to go to the doctor, he'd finally agreed. By the time they found out he had cancer, there wasn't much time left.

Those had been the hardest weeks of her life. Watching him suffer so, then slowly slip away. He'd felt so guilty that he was leaving her with all the responsibility of the lodge. She repeatedly told him she'd be fine. But the sad, tortured look in his eyes haunted her to this very day.

She'd tried to keep up a cheerful front for Beth and Jason, but they'd known what was happening. She wanted to give them a chance to say goodbye to their father, even if they were just young kids.

And Annie. Annie had been her savior, the only reason she hadn't completely fallen apart. Sitting at her side, holding her hand, when Ronnie ˉ finally slipped away and found his peace.

Ronnie's death had robbed her children of

their carefree childhood days. They'd both become more serious. Jason had tried bravely to be the man of the family, but he'd been just a young boy. Those years had been hard, so very hard. She'd struggled to make each and every payment to the bank, often going without any help at the lodge since there was no money to pay for help. Slowly, things had gotten a bit better, but she'd still struggled. Until Jason had come back from college and started helping her.

But now? All that would change. Their rustic, charming, quiet lodge would sit on the banks of a crowded, noisy lake.

She sighed again as she placed the photo back on the mantel. She kissed her fingers and touched them to the faded photo.

"I'll try to find a way, Ronnie. I will…"

CHAPTER 8

The next morning, Harrison headed into town to have that cup of coffee at Annie's... and to try and avoid the enticing aroma of a huge breakfast at the lodge. He'd dressed in the jeans and a flannel shirt he'd bought in Mountain Grove and felt almost like a regular Colorado type of guy. He pulled his car into a spot in front of Bookish Cafe and grabbed his sunglasses against the glare of the morning sunshine.

As he stepped out of the car and turned to enter the shop, he stopped dead in his tracks. There was Walt, lumbering down the sidewalk, not thirty feet from him. He'd recognize Walt anywhere. He'd put on weight, but he'd always been a big guy. Football lineman sized in high school, but more on the chubby side now.

A scowl covered Walt's reddened cheeks, and he hurried down the sidewalk, talking into this phone. "No, I need more time. It's not signed yet. No, I'll get it. I will."

Walt looked right at him, and Harrison caught his breath. But Walt didn't even miss a step as he hurried on past him.

He let out a long stream of air and turned to watch his cousin disappear down the street and head into city hall. Had Walt been talking about getting his mother's signature on the sale?

He chewed his bottom lip and turned around to get back in the car. If Walt was in town, he was going to take that opportunity to poke around the family property. He had every right to. His mother owned half the rights to it. With one last longing look at the bookstore and its promised cup of coffee, he climbed back into his car.

He pulled away from the curb and headed back to Lone Elk Lake. He drove past the cabin and pulled off in a clearing farther down the road where his car wouldn't be seen if Walt returned. He took an overgrown path through the woods. One he was surprised still existed. It had been the path from the cabin to an outcropping of rocks, farther down the lake's edge. Away from any direct sight of the cabin. Those rocks were where he and Walt and some of the boys from town had hung out for hours on end during the summer months. Well, he'd hung out with them when Walt invited him. Which wasn't very often.

He pushed through the overgrowth and slowed when he came to the clearing around the cabin. Memories crashed around him, and he just stood and stared at it. It looked exactly the same with its eclectic additions that somehow worked to make it look like a cohesive, sprawling cabin. The old barn at the edge of the property was badly in need of a coat of paint. He remembered spending one summer painting that barn alongside his grandfather. Walt was supposed to help them but rarely showed up, which had been fine with Harrison. He'd loved that time he'd spent one on one with his grandfather, talking about life, the future, the family's history.

He looked left and right, then stepped into the clearing, annoyed he felt guilty for walking on property he had every right to be on. Granted, Walt lived here now, rent-free it appeared in his research. And the family trust paid for the upkeep. Nice deal —for Walt.

He continued across the drive and went around to the lake side of the cabin and stopped abruptly.

There, standing on her tiptoes and peeking in the window, was Linda Seabridge.

"Hey." He hurried forward.

Her eyes flew open wide, and she stepped away from the window. "I—"

"What are you doing?"

"I'm just… I was on a walk… I saw this darling cabin."

"And decided to just come peek in the window of someone's home?"

She looked around guiltily. "I shouldn't have poked around, though." Then her eyes narrowed. "What are *you* doing here?"

Ah, the best defense was offense. But he didn't really know what to say to her without explaining who he was. "I was out walking around the lake and saw you peering in the windows." Almost the truth. Kind of.

She stepped away from the cabin. "I called out to see if anyone was home…"

"Really?" He doubted that.

"I'm interested in the property." She squared her shoulders.

"Somehow I doubt that's the real story."

"I don't owe you an explanation."

"Well, you could probably explain it to the sheriff…" He took a step closer, strangely protective of this cabin he hadn't set eyes on in what seemed like a million years.

"No, I'll leave. I didn't mean to bother anyone. I'm sorry."

He stared at her, unsure what to do. He should call the sheriff, but then he'd have to explain what *he* was doing here.

"I'll just continue on my walk… I didn't mean any harm."

He just nodded, and she turned and hurried away, back in the direction of the trail to the lodge. Now, on top of the strange feeling that he should know her, he was suspicious about why she was poking around the cabin.

He watched until he could no longer see her… and *she* could no longer see him. He climbed the deck stretching across the lakeside of the cabin and looked out at the familiar view. He ran his hand along the weathered knotty pine railing, connecting with the cabin and his past. The past came back and slammed over him. He had to clutch the rail to keep from tumbling. He took a deep breath, drawing in the present and exhaling the past.

He turned and crossed the wide plank flooring. Slowly he reached out and put his hand on the doorknob... but couldn't make himself actually twist the worn knob and open the door.

He reminded himself that he had every right to enter the cabin, but it still felt wrong since Walt actually lived here.

Dropping his hand, he turned back to look at the view again, lost in memories of the place, both good ones and... terrible ones.

CHAPTER 9

A nnie and Nora sat on a wide wooden swing on the porch of the main building at the lodge overlooking the lake. "I heard gossip in town that Walt just needs a signature and his sale of the land will go through. Some kind of hold up with some other family member signing the sale paper." Annie sighed. "It seems like no matter what we do, we're not going to be able to block this."

"There has to be a way. There has to." Nora couldn't imagine that the peace stretching out before her could explode in jet skis and a view of towering condos across the lake.

"The petition we started for the council to intervene and force the zoning committee to reconsider and hold community discussion on the issue is gaining signatures."

"But probably not enough, right?"

"Probably not." A sad look crossed her friend's face. "Do you think it's really going to hurt your business?"

Nora stared out at the lake. "Probably. I think our regulars will drop off, and I'll really miss that. We've had some of the same families coming here for over twenty years. I guess we'll get a new, younger crowd. And we do have the chalet now. That will keep us busy with weddings and meeting groups."

But it just won't be the same place. Sadness crept over her. She'd dealt with other difficult blows in life and weathered them. She'd weather this one, too. She just... well, she just didn't *want* to. She wanted things to stay the same. Her kids were happily married. Her grandkids were healthy. The lodge was finally turning a profit so they didn't have to struggle so much year by year.

She knew she should count her blessings, not focus on this one change. This one *major* change.

She turned at the sound of someone walking across the wooden planks of the porch.

"Good afternoon." Harrison stood in front

of them wearing much more appropriate clothing than his usual attire and looking at her with those crystal clear eyes of his. She shifted on the swing and it started moving.

"Hello, Harrison." Annie smiled at him.

"Uh, hi," Nora said oh so eloquently.

"You look like a real Coloradoan with those clothes. You look much more comfortable. We're not very fancy dressers here in Sweet River Falls." Annie steadied the swing with her foot.

Nora noticed he looked troubled, not that she knew what could possibly trouble a person on vacation in this beautiful town. Maybe he was avoiding something at home. Running away from something. Her imagination ran wild again for a moment, still thinking he'd given her a half-truth about why he was here in town, but she reined it back in. "Did you get them from Chuck at Alpine Outfitters?"

His eyes clouded momentarily, but then he shrugged. "I was out driving around, just exploring the area, and found a place in Mountain Grove."

Well, no matter where he'd found the clothes, they looked good on him. The jeans covered his long legs, and the flannel shirt stretched across his broad chest. Not that she was looking at his chest or his legs *or* his eyes…

Annie glanced at her, then stared at her closely and suppressed a grin. Nora glared at her. Annie shook her head, a smile teasing the corners of her mouth, and turned back to Harrison. "So, are you enjoying your stay in the area?"

"I am."

"I still owe you a cup of coffee," Annie offered.

"You mean for that one he dumped all over me?" Nora almost gasped, mortified she'd just blurted that out.

But she was reassured by the easy smile that flashed across his features. "Yes, that one. But if I hadn't run into you—literally—we might never have gotten to know each other."

Annie looked from Nora to Harrison and back to Nora. "I… should go. Got to get back to the shop."

"Don't leave on my account. I'm headed back to my cabin to get some work done." He nodded to them both, turned, and disappeared down the trail toward his cabin.

Anne shifted in the seat and stared at her. "So… what's up with *that*?"

"With what?" She still peered toward where Harrison had disappeared.

"You. Him." Annie didn't even try to hide her grin now. "I haven't seen you this flustered in… well, in a lot of years."

"I don't know what you're talking about," Nora lied.

Annie shook her head and stood. "Right. Just keep telling yourself that." With a quick wave, she disappeared too, a grin still spread across her face, leaving Nora alone and strangely out of sorts.

There was nothing between her and Harrison. He was just a guest at the lodge. Nothing more.

She scowled. She might as well try to believe that lie because she wasn't sure she was ready for anything more than that…

Nora looked around the dining hall that night, definitely *not* watching for Harrison. It was a busy Friday night, and most of the tables were full. As soon as they got one group finished and the table cleared off, another group sat down.

She didn't see Linda *Seabridge* either. She'd

finally looked the woman's last name up in the computer since she couldn't keep thinking of her as Linda-from-Baltimore.

No Linda. No Harrison. For a brief moment she wondered if they'd gone out together somewhere. She'd practically thrust them together last night. Maybe they'd hit it off. Maybe they'd gone out on a date.

Well, that was okay. They were free to date. It didn't matter to her one way or the other.

She shoved her imagination away and turned to greet another group of new customers. As she led them over to a table and handed them menus, she noticed Linda standing in the doorway.

Alone.

That answered that question.

She walked over and greeted her, tamping down the feeling of delight at seeing Linda here… *alone*. "Hi, just one?" Just to confirm…

"Yes, just one." Linda followed her to a table in the corner. "Looks like you're busy again tonight."

"We are. The lodge is full of people here for a wedding this weekend. The wedding party is having a small rehearsal dinner at the chalet, but a lot of their guests came for the weekend."

She didn't know why she was explaining all this to Linda. "I'll send your server over."

She headed across the room to find the waitress and spied Harrison standing in the doorway of the dining room, looking across the crowded tables. Her heart sped up, which annoyed her, so she ignored it. She calmly, *ever so calmly*, walked up to him. "Hello, again."

He gave her a warm smile. That wasn't helping her determinedly calm state of mind. "Hi."

"I just sat Linda Seabridge. I could see if she'd mind you joining her." Now why had she offered that?

A brief frown crossed his face. "No, I... ah... I think I'd prefer to dine alone tonight."

A smile tugged at the corners of her mouth. "I have a table right by the windows if you'd like that."

"I'd love that. I do enjoy looking out at the view."

She was acutely aware of him following her across the room, just steps behind her. She paused when a server crossed in front of them, and Harrison gently bumped into her.

"Oops, sorry."

"No problem." She choked the words out

and led him to a table, then reluctantly went back to work.

Harrison lingered over his meal, not that she noticed. She dropped by his table after his dinner was cleared away.

"Do you want another glass of wine?"

"If I say yes, would you join me?"

She looked around the room. They were still busy tonight. "I'd like to, but I really need to keep working."

"Maybe some other time, then."

Was that a look of disappointment on his face?

She was imagining things.

He got up from the table. "Another wonderful meal. I'm going to gain ten pounds if I keep eating like this."

He turned and walked out of the dining room, and she watched every single step he took. She turned as a waitress called her name.

Back to work. If only they'd been a bit slower tonight and she could have joined him for that glass of wine.

And that was the first time she'd ever wished things were *less* busy at the lodge.

CHAPTER 10

Harrison headed out from the dining room and wandered down to the lake as his eyes adjusted to the night. Moonlight illuminated the path. He glanced up toward the night sky. It looked like almost a full moon. He leaned over and picked up a rock and skipped it across the surface. He grinned in spite of himself. He hadn't done that since he was a boy. His grandfather had taught him how to do it one summer when he was about six. He'd probably skipped a million rocks across this lake, no lie.

He picked up another one and skipped it. Three hops this time.

About a dozen rocks later he gave up trying to get four hops out of a rock. He looked across the lake and saw faint lighting coming from the windows of his grandfather's cabin. Well, Walt's cabin.

No, it wasn't *Walt's* cabin, he reminded himself. Walt had just taken on squatter's rights, without asking anyone else in the family.

First thing Monday he was going to visit county records and look for the original deed to the place and any transfers or amendments. This afternoon, after his adventure of visiting the cabin, he'd tried to get in contact with the law firm that did his grandfather's estate. They'd had an honest-to-goodness *gone fishing* sign in the window. A man from the neighboring office had said Friday afternoons were usually a fishing day for the lawyer who ran the practice now.

Small towns. They sure were different than Chicago. He couldn't remember the last time he'd left early on a Friday from his job.

Or the last time he'd gone fishing, for that matter. Maybe he'd find time to drop a line in the lake while he was here.

He walked along the trail that ran beside the lake and stopped at a boulder by the edge. He scrambled onto it and looked across the water. It was a nice night out, and he was plenty warm with just a light jacket over his flannel shirt. He looked up at the vast array of stars flung across the sky above him. No view like this in Chicago either. He'd actually moved to a condo downtown about ten years ago to be nearer to his work. Yep, no skies like this in downtown Chicago.

The peace of the evening settled around him. An owl hooted from a nearby tree. The fresh scent of pine wrapped around him.

And he just… sat.

When was the last time he'd just sat and listened to the silence? It was a peaceful almost-silence. He could hear some creature, a squirrel or chipmunk, rustle along the ground in the leaves beside the trail. The owl called out a melancholy hoot again. The breeze ruffled the leaves on the trees in a soothing lullaby of quiet whispers.

He sat there and soaked in the beauty and ambience of the lake. He was certain there was no place like this in all of the world and regretted all the years he'd stayed away. Not that he'd really had any choice.

NORA HEADED BACK to her cabin, her mind on

tomorrow's wedding at the lodge and all that still needed to be done. Luckily she had Bree and Cece to do most of it. Hiring the Stuart sisters had taken a load off her shoulders on wedding weekends. Her mind bounced on to Harrison. He intrigued her with his quick smile and his easy conversation. She could relax and be herself with him, and yet, in some ways, he unsettled her.

She paused as she noticed someone sitting on a boulder at the edge of the lake. Her *favorite* boulder for lake watching, actually.

In an instant, she knew who it was.

Harrison. Had she conjured him up from her thoughts? She pushed the silly notion aside.

She could cross over to another trail that led to the river path and leave him to his lake watching. And yet… she didn't.

She continued down the trail and paused near the boulder. "Hi." Her voice was low so as not to startle him.

He turned to her, and she saw his smile, welcoming her in the moonlight. "Well, this is a nice surprise. Care to join me?" He reached out a hand and motioned to the rock beside him.

"I…" *Should she?* Yes, yes she should. She wanted to. "I'd like that." She climbed up beside him on the large, smooth rock. "This is my favorite place to sit and look over the lake. A bit away from everything. So peaceful."

"It is a nice spot. I can see why it's your favorite. And look at those stars." He flung his arm above him. "We don't have those stars in Chicago."

She grinned at him. "Well, you do have those stars, you just can't see them very well through the light pollution."

"Point taken." He stared up at the sky. "It seems so endless and majestic. I remember seeing skies like this as a boy."

"Really? Where?"

He glanced at her, and a quick frown floated across his features and left just as quickly. "Oh, here and there on vacations with my folks."

"Always nice to get out of the city for a bit."

"It is." He leaned back on his elbows and stretched his legs in front of him. "I can't imagine having this view for the taking, every single day."

She looked up at the familiar sky. It was a blessing to have this view. The sky. The mountains. The lake. She was a very lucky woman. And she never took it for granted.

Harrison sat back up. "So... this Dobbs guy you spoke of. He's going to change all this?"

"Well, yes. Across the way there..." She pointed across the lake. "That's where he plans on putting in condos. Lots of condos. Along with lots of condos will come lots of light, so the sky view won't be the same."

"And he wants to allow motorboats on the lake?"

"He does. Right now we have canoes, kayaks, an occasional small sailboat. That's it."

"It seems... wrong. Why did the city council allow it?"

"Because Dobbs gets what he wants in this town. Almost always. He has friends in power and... well, he usually wins. We did get the riverwalk put in behind the buildings on Main Street along Sweet River. He didn't want that."

"Why not?"

"Maybe because he didn't think of the idea? Maybe because Annie and I worked so hard to get it passed through the town council?"

A deep frown creased his features. "Sounds like this Dobbs is quite a character."

She couldn't agree with him more. They sat in silence for a while, looking at the stars. Listening to the gentle evening sounds. She finally sighed. "I should probably go. Long day tomorrow with a wedding at the lodge."

"I should probably head in, too. May I walk you back to your cabin?"

"That would be nice." She stood and climbed off the rock. She led him over to the trail that crossed to the river. The moonlight lit their way.

"You walk home alone every night?"

"Most nights. Occasionally I drive to the lodge if it's raining. But more likely I just grab an umbrella. I love this walk to start my day and end my day."

"It sounds like a fine way to begin and end a day." They continued along the path until they got to her cabin and climbed the familiar stairs to the porch. And yet they felt strangely different with Harrison beside her.

"Well, thanks for walking me home. You sure you know your way back?"

"I've got it. And the moon is bright enough. I'm good."

She stood there for a moment, looking at his chiseled face in the soft light filtering through the windows. She placed her hand on the knob. "I should go in."

"Goodnight, then." He turned away.

She turned the knob and stepped through the door.

"Nora?"

She turned back to look at him. "Yes?"

"I… I like talking to you." He shifted from foot to foot. "You're… easy to talk to, and I've enjoyed spending time with you."

She didn't know what to say to that. She'd enjoyed spending time with him, too.

"How would you like to… well, go out with me? I know you're busy tomorrow with the wedding, but maybe on Sunday? We could go into town to eat. Maybe grab lunch?"

"That sounds nice." Her heart did a double beat.

"Perfect. I'll meet you here? Or at the lodge? Noonish?"

"How about meeting at the lodge?"

"See you then." He turned and walked away, and she watched him disappear down the trail beside the river.

Had he just asked her on a date? Was she, Nora Cassidy, going on a real live date? Annie was *never* going to believe this…

CHAPTER 11

Nora left early the next morning to head to the lodge. It was non-stop activity throughout the day with people staying at the lodge for the wedding, along with other guests arriving late afternoon.

She hurried along the pathway to the chalet, her arms full of a basket of a selection of crackers. Bree had called back to the lodge and said they were running low on crackers to go with the variety of cheeses set out for appetizers.

She ducked in the back entrance to the kitchen of the chalet. "Here you go." She handed the crackers to Bree.

"Thank you so much. I don't know what happened to the crackers. I'm usually more organized than this."

"It was no problem." She smiled at her new daughter-in-law. Daughter-in-law. The words rolled unfamiliarly through her mind. She couldn't quite get used to the idea that Jason was married now. Happily married. It had been quite a year. A lot of changes.

And now Harrison... She shook her head and glanced around at the people bustling around the kitchen. "Everything going okay?"

"Everything is great. The ceremony went fine, of course, with Cece in charge. We're serving drinks and appetizers while the bride and groom get pictures taken. Then later, there's the buffet dinner."

"Looks like you have it all covered."

Cece popped her head into the kitchen. "Oh, hey, Nora."

"Hi, Cece. I hear the ceremony went well."

"It was lovely." Cece nodded and turned to Bree. "Bartender needs more ice at the bar. Want me to get it?"

"Here, I'll take it out." She might as well make herself useful while she was here.

"Thanks, Nora." Cece disappeared back out of the kitchen.

Nora went to the freezer, took out some more ice, and placed it in an ice bin.

"Thanks, Nora." Bree turned to set up a tray with the newly acquired crackers.

Nora pushed through the kitchen door, walked through the chalet, and out onto the deck on the lakeside where the bar had been set up. She handed the ice to the bartender and turned to leave.

"Well, Nora. What are you doing here dressed like that? So inappropriate." Gloria Edmonds, dressed in a tailored navy dress that look like it had been expressly made for her—and it probably had—stood directly in her path.

"Hello, Gloria." She'd learned long ago to ignore Gloria's remarks. Mostly.

"Do you know you're out of ice?"

"Just brought out some more." She gritted her teeth, reminding herself that Gloria was obviously a guest of the wedding, so therefore she needed to be civil to her.

Gloria clung to the arm of Mr. Ashbury, father of the bride. Gloria turned to him. "I thought there might be some problems like this when you said your daughter was getting married *here*, of all places. Even though they built this little building… well… the whole setting is so rustic, and well, things like *this* happen.

Nora wasn't sure if she was the *this* that happened, or the fact the ice had been out for all of like three minutes. Well, it hadn't even been out, just *almost* out. *And* she shouldn't have to defend herself or her beloved lodge to Gloria Edmonds.

"This is Mr. Ashbury." Gloria beamed at the man and practically fluttered her eyelashes.

"Yes, we've met." They'd met when he'd come to see the venue with his daughter.

"I think it's a wonderful venue, and my daughter has been so pleased with everything. From the food, the flowers, the fabulous view." Mr. Ashbury smiled at Nora.

His words vindicated her.

Gloria frowned. "Well… I guess. It is a shame that the Bellingham didn't have any availability for her."

The Bellingham—the new, elegant, chic hotel right outside of town. A whole different vibe than the chalet here at the lodge. She ignored Gloria's remark. Mostly.

"Maybe when the condo complex gets built on Walter's property, we'll have more choices of venues around here. They'll probably put in a big community area with it. Hopefully, the complex will give people another *suitable* choice at the lake."

"Nice to see you, Gloria," Nora lied. "I should get back to the lodge." Truth. She should get back to the lodge before she strangled Gloria. The woman got under her skin every single time she saw her. And it annoyed her to no end that she let the woman get to her.

"Well, my daughter is having a wonderful wedding here. Thank you so much." Mr. Ashbury glanced over at his daughter, standing by the lake with her new husband while the photographer posed them for a photo with the sunset in the background. "Everything has been perfect."

"We like to hear that." She smiled at him— not at Gloria—and turned away.

"I hope your daughter isn't going to get her lovely dress all dirty down by the lake..." Gloria's words drifted across the breeze as she hurried away.

And she *mostly* ignored them...

CHAPTER 12

The next day Nora put on clean jeans and a bright coral sweater. She looked in the mirror and decided to put on a touch of makeup, something she rarely did. She was ridiculously nervous, which was *ridiculous* in and of itself.

She was just going out to lunch with Harrison. No big deal.

Keep repeating that and maybe she'd believe it.

She took one last glance in the mirror, tucked her hair behind her ear and then untucked it. She frowned when she looked closely in the mirror. When had she gotten those small wrinkles at the corners of her eyes? And it always surprised her to see the subtle streaks of gray in her hair. Not that she really minded getting older. Usually. She didn't *feel* her age. Well, most days she didn't. Growing older was a strange process…

And Harrison had asked her out. He'd seen the real her and still asked her on a date. She sighed and messed with her hair again.

Enough.

With a shrug, she turned and left, heading for the lodge. There was still lots on her to-do list to finish before her lunch with Harrison. And the busier she kept, the less nervous she'd be.

Maybe.

She walked along the river, and its soothing melody did calm her nerves. She couldn't remember the last time she'd been on a date, much less a date with someone who actually intrigued her. She was always too busy with running the lodge, or helping Beth with the boys, or just… life. And she was perfectly happy the way her life was now. She didn't really need the complication of a date.

But it couldn't hurt anything, could it?

She cut over to the lake and walked along the trail. She was later than usual this morning, and a few of the guests were out sitting by the lake, sipping coffee. She glanced at her watch. How had it gotten this late?

She knew how it happened. It was the twenty minutes of deciding what to wear, then the time to put on makeup and mess with her hair.

She hurried into the kitchen at the lodge, hoping that Judy would give her a long list of tasks to do to help with the breakfast rush.

HARRISON PULLED on a pair of his new jeans, wishing he'd had time to wash them so they weren't so stiff. He should have thrown all the new clothes in the washer. He'd seen the lodge had a laundry area for the guests to use. He dug through the flannel shirts he bought but then decided to simply put on a light blue button-down shirt he'd brought with him from Chicago.

He rolled up the sleeves. Then rolled them back down. Then rolled them back up.

A long sigh escaped his lips. Why in the world would a simple lunch with Nora make him act like a nervous teenager? Not that he'd ever dated as a teen. He'd been the out-of-shape nerd.

He glanced down at his hard-won flat stomach. He really was going to go to the gym and get back on a diet... as soon as he left Sweet River Falls.

He glanced at his cell phone. It was only eleven-thirty. Maybe if he walked really, *really* slowly, it would take him ten minutes or so to walk to the lodge. No, he needed to take his vehicle so he could drive them into town.

He walked out onto the wide porch overlooking the lake. A slight breeze ruffled the surface of the water. The not-quite-noon sun bounced reflections of sunlight across the distance. He paced to the end of the deck. Then back again, glancing at his rolled-up sleeves. He forced himself to leave them rolled up.

He stared across the lake to the distant shore. He could see a couple of people walking along the shoreline in front of his grandfather's cabin. It was too far to make out if one of them was Walt or not.

He jammed his fingers through his hair in aggravation. Walt. Always up to something and always looking out for his own best interests. He was positive by now that Walt was not giving his mother her fair share if indeed the sale went through. He had more research to do.

Then he was going to confront Walt.

He snagged his phone from his pocket to check the time. Should be okay to drive on over to the lodge now. He could be a tiny bit fashionably early, right?

At precisely ten until noon, he sat in his car in front of the dining lodge. Should he go on in? Wait until noon? He rolled his eyes at himself and opened the car door.

Just go inside, you fool.

He ran into Mac with two young boys on the porch to the lodge.

"Hey, Harrison. Good to see you."

"Mac." They shook hands.

"This is Connor and Trevor."

"How come Connor always gets introduced first?" The younger boy tugged on Mac's arm.

"Sorry about that. This is *Trevor* and Connor." Mac grinned.

"Mac's our new stepdad," Trevor announced.

"Nice to meet you, Trevor and Connor."

"We're just headed out to go hiking. Great day for it, don't you think?" Mac rested a hand casually on each boy's shoulder.

"Does look like it."

"Mom is helping at the lodge today. Grams has a date," Connor added.

Harrison hid a smile. "She does, does she?"

"Yep, and Mom says Grams *never* dates."

He tucked that tiny piece of information away.

Mac grinned. "We should go before... well, no secrets with these two around. Have a good time."

The trio left and Harrison walked into the main room of the lodge, strangely comforted by the fact it appeared Nora didn't date often either.

CHAPTER 13

Nora looked up to see Harrison standing just inside the front door of the lodge. She watched as his gaze swept the room until he saw her. She lifted a hand in a wave, and he hurried toward her.

Where had the time gone? She'd wanted to jump into the ladies' room for one last look at her hair and makeup. But that was ridiculous, too. Since when did she worry about things like that? So much ridiculousness swirling around her today.

"You ready?" Harrison gave her one of his disarming smiles.

A smile that she tried her best to *not* let disarm her.

"I am." She turned to Jason. "I'll be back later this afternoon."

"Take as long as you want. We've got things covered here. You two have fun." Jason turned to wait on a guest.

"Looks like I'm good to go." Nora walked out from behind the reception desk.

"So where would you like to go? You're the expert on the area."

"Well, if you don't mind a drive, there's an old inn about halfway up Sky View Mountain. Harmony Haven Inn. It's got a wonderful view. They have delightful luncheons on Sundays. Salad bar, fresh soups, and homemade bread. And the desserts are to die for."

"That sounds great. Harmony Haven Inn it is."

She climbed into his low-slung sports car with less grace than she would have liked and gave him directions to the inn.

He carefully drove up the switchbacks on the country road that led up the mountain. She looked out at the view as they climbed higher. She should be pointing out things in the view, or chatting, or something. But words escaped her. Which was *ridiculous*, but she was beginning to expect ridiculous when she was around

Harrison. They finally reached the turnoff, and they pulled into the parking lot in front of the inn.

The rustic pine logs of the exterior were kept in perfect condition. A bright red roof contrasted against the green of the pine trees behind the inn. She loved this place but rarely made time to get away and enjoy it. It had probably been five years or so since she'd been here. She didn't know why she didn't make it a point to come here more often. Well, yes, she did. She was always so darn busy with the lodge.

Harrison opened the car door and held out a hand. She slipped her hand into his and he firmly clasped it, his fingers strong around hers as he helped her out of the car. With just a tiny bit more grace than when she'd clambered into the car.

"This place is amazing." Harrison was looking all around. "The view is... well... breathtaking."

"It is, isn't it? You can see the town of Sweet River Falls all nestled in the valley. The inn has been owned by the Harmon family for three generations. They do lunch and dinner during the week, then this fabulous buffet on the weekends. Not to be missed."

"Oh, I get it. Harmon family—Harmony Haven Inn."

"Yep, that's how it got its name."

They climbed the steep stairs to enter the inn. A smiling hostess sat them at a pine table, polished to a sparkling finish. The table was right next to the window, and Harrison gasped when he sat down. "The view is even more fabulous from here if that's even possible."

She smiled. "I thought you might like this place. And just wait till you taste the food. It's even more amazing than the view."

He grinned. "It's going to take quite a bit to outdo that cook you have at your lodge."

"Trust me. We're not even in the same league as Evie Harmon."

The waitress took their drink order, and they went to fill their plates at the buffet. Nora was slightly embarrassed at the amount of food she took. Homemade vegetable soup, fresh baked bread, a salad with homemade croutons, and a slice of beef *and* a slice of ham. And she knew she wasn't going to turn down a piece of pie for dessert, either.

When they sat down, she was glad to see that Harrison had taken even more food than she had.

The conversation flowed easily as they ate the delicious meal. Harrison asked a lot of questions about Lone Elk Lake and the people and businesses on it as well as questions about the town council. He questioned her about real estate values of property on the lake. It crossed her mind that he might be considering buying a place in the area, and that thought pleased her.

They finished eating their meal while chatting about the town, the view, her grandsons, and the food. Lots of talk about the incredible food.

Harrison ended his meal with a piece of pecan pie, and she had a slice of apple pie. When they finally finished, he pushed away from the table. "I'm never going to eat again."

"Right." She grinned at him.

"No, seriously. You guys are killing me. I've eaten more since I've come to Sweet River Falls than I've had in months and months of meals." He placed his napkin on the table. "But you are so right. That is one of the best meals I've ever eaten, no offense to the wonderful food you serve at the lodge."

"The Harmon family guards their recipes like a hawk. I've tried to replicate their blueberry muffins to no avail. And I don't even try to compete with that pecan pie."

"Pretty sure nothing would compete with it."

She leaned back in her chair, just enjoying their time together. She was surprised at how relaxed she'd been and how all her nervousness had just faded away. She'd really enjoyed their lunch and wasn't ready for the date to end.

"Do you want to walk off some of your meal?" She looked at him lazing across from her, his long legs stretched under the table and brushing against hers. Not that she'd noticed.

"That's probably a good idea. But I'd need to hike all the way down the mountain and back up to walk off all of that meal."

"There's a trail at the end of the parking lot that takes you to an overlook of the valley if you'd like to see it. You can actually see Lone Elk Lake from up there."

"Then it sounds like a plan." Harrison paid their bill, and they walked out into the sunny afternoon.

Bright blue skies stretched above them, and large, fluffy white clouds drifted in the breeze. She lifted her face toward the warmth of the sun.

Harrison looked over at Nora, with her face tilted up toward the warm afternoon sunshine.

He wanted to reach out and tilt her face just slightly more and kiss those lips of hers…

What?

Where had *that* thought come from?

She stood in the sunshine oblivious to his thoughts. She finally opened her eyes and turned toward him. "I do love a sunny fall day." She shrugged, unabashed at being caught just standing and soaking up the rays. "Though my favorite is the very first snowfall of the year. There's just something so special about it. We haven't had snow yet this year."

He was sorry that he wasn't going to be here to share the first snowfall with her. And *that* thought bothered him, too.

"Okay, it's this way." She started across the parking area.

He stood like a statue, still processing his thoughts.

She looked back over her shoulder. "You coming?"

He trotted to catch up with her, tucking his

thoughts of kissing her firmly away from his mind. Mostly.

They slowly made their way along the path, threading their way through the tall pines and in and out of splashes of sunshine. They finally came to an outcropping of rocks, and Nora spread her arms wide. "Behold, the best view of Sweet River Falls and the surrounding area."

He tore his gaze from her and looked down at the view. He pointed. "Is that Lone Elk Lake over there?"

"It is."

"And I can see where the Sweet River comes into the valley, too."

"Yep."

"I have to agree, this is the best view. Even though I thought the one from the parking lot was the best until I got to the one from the dining room in the inn. But this view does win."

"Told you." A satisfied grin crossed her face.

"Well, you obviously know what you're talking about when it comes to panoramic views."

"Stick around a while and I'll show you some of the best views in the whole state." She looked at him quickly as if surprised she'd said that. "Oh, I know you're leaving soon. But... I mean…" She stumbled over her words. "Well, there are a lot of wonderful places around here."

He couldn't imagine a place more wonderful than this one, right here, with Nora. But he wasn't going to pass up an opportunity to spend even more time with her. "I'd like it if you can get away from work again and show me another of your best-in-state views. Think we could arrange that?"

Nora looked out over the valley as if deciding on what to answer. But then she'd been the one to suggest another outing. Still, she paused. She finally turned and looked directly at him. "I think that I can find some time to show you around."

Her face was flushed a bit, but he couldn't tell if it was from the exertion from the hike to this lookout point, or something else. He had to tell himself to quit staring at her lips.

She stood there, just looking at him, and in spite of telling himself not to, he reached out and brushed a lock of her hair away from her face. Her eyes widened and a flicker of… something… Desire?… flashed through them.

He was a goner then. Didn't matter how much his head said to step back, he ignored it and leaned forward and kissed her, ever so slowly. Her hand came to rest on his chest, and he covered it with his own. He could have stood there kissing her forever.

He finally pulled back and looked at her. Her amber eyes shined brightly, and now her cheeks were a rosy red, and he was certain *that* wasn't from their hike.

"I… um…" She looked directly into his eyes. "I wasn't expecting that."

He grinned. "I wasn't either." He still held her hand against him and debated kissing her again.

She looked at her hand pressing against his chest as if surprised to see it resting there, then slowly pulled it away. The heat still burned through him where her hand had just been.

"I should probably get back." Nora turned to look out at the view again, her hands firmly slipped in her pockets now.

He reached over and gently turned her face to look at him. "I wasn't expecting that kiss either, but I'm really glad it happened."

CHAPTER 14

Nora sat on a rock beside Sweet River outside her cabin late that night. She'd been pretty worthless as help in the kitchen at the lodge for dinner. Judy had finally shooed her away. She'd gone to her office to catch up on paperwork but found herself staring out the window. She'd finally given up and headed back to her cabin, but after a few minutes in the cabin, the air had felt stifling, and she'd gone to sit outside.

She sat and waited for the night to bring her the peace it usually did. To wrap around her and soothe her.

But tonight, the night didn't do its usual magic.

So many thoughts twisted through her mind. The kiss, of course. How Harrison's eyes had glistened with desire as he leaned in to kiss her. She'd only realized he was going to kiss her about a half-second before he did. Not enough time to decide if she should step back. Not enough time to decide if she wanted the kiss.

But she had wanted him to kiss her. She had.

But the kiss... it had rocked her to her very core. Emotions had awakened in her that she never thought she'd have again. Crashing over her and making her feel so... alive.

And now, back at the cabin she'd shared with Ronnie... there was also a feeling of guilt and regret. Like she was cheating on her husband. Which was ridiculous—why was Harrison always making her have *ridiculous* thoughts—because Ronnie had been gone for so many years. He would have wanted her to move on, to be happy. But still, there was that tiny nagging guilt that swirled around her. It had caught her by surprise to feel this guilt after all this time.

She touched her lips, trailing a finger across them, still feeling Harrison's kiss.

She looked up at the night sky. "Ronnie, I don't know what to do. I'm sorry. And I miss you. I miss you so very much."

But, of course, Ronnie didn't answer.

CHAPTER 15

Nora headed to Annie's first thing after the breakfast rush at the lodge. Talking to Annie was the only way to sort out her emotions. Her friend would talk her through it. She always did.

Annie was sweeping the sidewalk outside Bookish Cafe. "Nora, this is a surprise." Annie stopped and frowned. "What's wrong?"

"Nothing." Nora shrugged.

"Yes, there is. Come inside and have some coffee with me. We'll talk."

Nora was grateful for her friend's intuition. Annie never let her down. They settled upstairs in the loft with two steaming mugs of coffee.

"Now, talk to me." Annie gave her a don't-argue look.

"I… well, I went out with Harrison yesterday."

Annie looked surprised. "You did? Why didn't you tell me?"

"I…" She shrugged again. "I don't know. I felt… silly? I got all nervous like a young girl going on her first date."

"That's exactly *why* you should have told me. Anyway, tell me more."

"We went to Harmony Haven Inn and had their brunch."

"And?"

"And we had a good time. He loved the place, but then, everyone does. Then we walked over to lookout point."

"Best view of Sweet River Falls ever." Annie nodded.

"And then…" She paused and looked down at her coffee as if it held the answer to everything.

"And then what? Don't make me drag it out of you."

"He… he kissed me." Her voice was barely a whisper.

A huge smile spread across Annie's face. "Well, good for him. I *knew* there was something going on between the two of you."

"No, there isn't." But of course, there was *something* going on.

Annie's eyes narrowed. "You okay?"

She looked at her friend. "Of course I am."

"But you don't know how you're really feeling about all of this, do you?"

Annie was always so on point.

"I… I don't. I mean I've enjoyed spending time with him. He's easy to talk to and I like spending time with him."

"But… Ronnie. It's Ronnie, isn't it?"

Nora sighed. "I know it's ridiculous to feel guilty about kissing someone this long after Ronnie's death, but I… well, I *do* feel slightly guilty. Like I'm cheating on him in some way."

"I'm not going to say that's ridiculous. It's just how you feel." Annie reached over and squeezed her hand. "Love is complicated."

"I don't *love* Harrison."

"But you loved Ronnie with all your heart. And I know you still miss him every single day. It's only logical that feelings for Harrison are going to be complicated. I think you need to give yourself a break while you sort it all out. And… don't push him away. I mean it." Annie gave her another of her world-famous you-better-listen-to-me stares.

Nora turned and looked out the window at the soothing ripples of Sweet River as it rushed over the tumbled stones. Annie was right, of course. She did need to give herself a break and take some time to sort everything out. It just felt so incredibly strange to have feelings for another man.

Whatever those actual feelings might be. She wasn't quite ready to label them yet.

Harrison spent the morning pacing his cabin. Wishing he'd kissed Nora again when he dropped her off at the lodge. Or again at the overlook. Or… well, any time. The kiss had affected him in ways he could hardly process. Though he thought with the million times he'd gone over the kiss in his mind, he'd have figured out his emotions by now. Nora moved him and had awakened emotions he was unfamiliar with, and he wasn't sure he liked that. He wanted control back. For that matter, he wanted control back over everything. His life, this mess with the cabin and property, *and* his emotions.

Maybe it was coming back to this town, a place that had meant so much to him in the past. Maybe it was slowing down and taking time to just breathe. Maybe... maybe he had feelings for Nora.

Maybe.

He put the thoughts aside and drove into town for an eleven o'clock appointment with the estate lawyer—after calling to make sure the lawyer wasn't 'gone fishing' again today.

The young lawyer greeted him when he entered. "So, you want information on your grandfather's will?"

"I have a copy of his original will. But my mother seems to think Grandfather made a new will sometime after that. She said she remembers him talking to her about it."

"Is there a problem with the estate?" He took a seat behind his desk and motioned for Harrison to sit as well.

"No, not a problem. Just... trying to figure some things out." Harrison took the offered chair across from the big, old wooden desk. Quite a contrast to the sleek, modern desk Harrison had back at his own office. And suddenly, he wanted an old desk like this. One with history. One where the wood was worn smooth by use. And a vivid image of his grandfather's old desk in the study at the cabin flashed into his mind.

Where were these strange thoughts coming from? He pulled his thoughts back to the matter at hand.

"I pulled your grandfather's file when you called this morning," the lawyer said. "It looks like my father drew up an amended trust for your grandfather. The will says that when he died, the property goes to the trust. I read through the original will and the original trust documents, but I don't have a copy of the amended trust for some reason. Just my father's notes that he was amending it. It's a bit strange that there's not a copy in the file."

"Do you know what changed?" Harrison frowned.

"No, not exactly. I don't think it could have been changed much. There's a note in here about descendants. That's about all. And there's a copy of the bill for Dad's services, and it wasn't much. So I don't think it was a total rewrite. Doesn't anyone in your family have a copy of the trust agreement?"

"Not that I know of."

The lawyer looked at him. "Is this about Walter wanting to sell the cabin and the property? I know he got the area rezoned, and rumor has it he's got a buyer who wants to put up condos."

"So I've heard."

"Is there a problem?"

Other than the fact that his mother wasn't going to want to sign on the sale if she heard that the property was going to be sold for condos and probably the cabin torn down in the process? Or that feeling that Walt wasn't giving his mother a fair deal?

"That's what I'm trying to find out. Thanks for your time." Harrison stood.

Time to do more digging around and find out just what Walt was up to.

And, just as importantly, he also wanted to go and find Nora. It was time he told her why he was really in town. Now that they'd gotten close, he didn't want them to have any secrets.

Annie walked Nora outside after their chat. Nora felt better after talking to Annie, which didn't surprise her. Her friend had a way of always making her feel better.

"You call me if you want to talk some more." Annie stood outside beside the door.

"I will. But I'm fine, really."

Annie didn't look convinced.

"I *will* be fine. Just need some time to sort things out."

"You mean admit you care about Harrison."

"I don't——" Nora glanced behind Annie. "Sh! He's coming down the sidewalk."

"Who? Harrison?" Annie turned, and a wide smile spread across her face. She waved to him. "Hey, Harrison."

He looked up and smiled back. "Hello, ladies."

"You coming for that cup of coffee I promised you?"

"I was actually looking for——" He paused, a look of surprise on his face as he studied the sidewalk behind them.

Nora turned to see what had drawn his attention. Walter Dobbs came lumbering toward them, waving a sheaf of paper in his hands, and he didn't look happy.

"Nora, what is this nonsense? Trying to get signatures to have the town council——" Walter stopped mid-sentence.

Did no man know how to finish their sentences in this town?

"Harrison?" Walter stilled the waving

papers, and a frown creased his face. "It *is* you, isn't it?"

"Walt." Harrison's voice was flat.

Nora looked from Harrison to Dobbs and back to Harrison. "You two know each other?"

"I'll say." Walt clapped Harrison on the back like they were old friends. "This here is my cousin."

Nora took a step back. Harrison and Dobbs were cousins? She glanced at Harrison, but he still looked a bit stunned.

"I didn't know you were in town. Why didn't you tell me? Why aren't you staying at the cabin? Plenty of room." Walt grabbed Harrison's hand and pumped it in greeting.

Harrison recovered. "I'm staying at the lodge, didn't want to impose. Just got to town."

Nora looked at Harrison. As if a week was considered *just* getting to town...

"Well, okay. But the offer still stands. Why don't you at least come over for drinks this evening? We can get caught up. Say, how is Aunt Ellen doing? Did she get those papers I sent her?"

"She did." Harrison's voice was tight and his eyes narrowed.

"Well, good, good. Let's see if we can get this business all wrapped up."

Her mind swirled with information and confusion. She turned to Harrison. "You and Walter are *cousins*?"

"Sure are." Walter nodded vigorously.

"But you're not a Dobbs."

"His mother is. His mother and my father were siblings." Walter grinned his politically correct grin that didn't quite reach his eyes.

"So…" She stood tall, anger racing through her. She balled her hands into fists. "So you've come to town to sign the papers to sell the Dobbs property? *That's* why you're here?" She felt Annie's hand on her arm in silent support. "All this time… it wasn't about…" She stopped herself before she said it wasn't about *her*. She'd been foolish enough. "You're just here to learn about selling your property? *That's* why you asked me out. *That's* why you asked so many questions about the lake and the town. You acted all interested and charming, but you were just *using* me."

He wasn't interested in *her*. He was here to sell the land and let the condo complex take over the lake. Heck, he probably had a motorboat he wanted to launch on the lake.

She'd been such a naive fool. And she didn't suffer fools lightly.

"Nora, no, it's not like that." He could see the anger plainly etched on her face. And he couldn't blame her. It did kind of seem like he'd set out to trick her. But he hadn't. He just wanted to learn all he could before Walt found out he was in town. And for Pete's sake, he'd been on his way *right now* to tell her why he was here.

"I—"

Nora held up a hand. "Don't bother. When I asked you why you were in town? *That* would have been a good time to tell me the truth."

"I know, I should have, but—"

"I don't want to hear it. I can't abide by liars. Especially ones who deliberately set out to deceive me. No wonder you asked so many questions about the lake and the town."

"Nora—"

She held up her hand again. "Don't." She turned to Annie. "I'm headed back to the lodge."

With that, she turned around and stalked off

down the sidewalk, the unmistakable set of her shoulders and the firmness of her steps telling him all he needed to know about how she felt about him.

Annie turned to him, and for the first time he saw a decidedly unfriendly look on her face. "I'm so disappointed. I just didn't expect this from you. Nora was beginning to... well, never mind. I'm going back to work." With that. she slipped into Bookish Cafe.

He guessed the offered cup of coffee was off the table now. He sighed, angry at himself for making such a mess of things.

Walt looked at him. "You went out with Nora? That was a mistake. She's nothing but trouble." He shook his head. "Anyway, you want to come over for that drink this evening?"

"Sure, why not?"

He watched while Walt headed down the sidewalk. Walt, all friendly and chummy like they'd actually been friends. Like what had happened all those years ago hadn't really happened.

He stood alone on the sidewalk and raked his hands through his hair. He'd messed this one up. His timing was terrible. If only he could've explained things to her before they ran into

Walt. Just when he'd started to have feelings for Nora. Exactly what feelings, he wasn't quite sure, but he'd hoped to find out.

Not much chance of that now, and he didn't blame her a bit.

Walt always had a way of screwing up his life.

He sighed. Okay, this time he had to take some of the blame for this mess himself.

CHAPTER 16

"Mom, you here?" Nora turned from the stack of dishes in the sink at the sound of Beth's voice. She sighed and put on a smile. No use dragging anyone else into her troubles. Annie had called twice, but Nora hadn't answered. She just didn't feel like talking to anyone right now. But Beth was here, so she'd pretend.

"In the kitchen." She reached for a towel to dry her hands. She'd come home from her run-in with Harrison and decided it was time to wash every glass in her kitchen. She'd almost completed the task and was considering washing windows next...

Beth entered the kitchen and dropped her

purse and jacket on a chair. "So… how did it go?"

"How did what go?"

"Mom! Your date with Harrison yesterday. I want details. Well, not *all* the details. Just some of them."

"It was fine. We went to Harmony Haven Inn and had a nice brunch."

"And that's all? Did he ask you out again?"

"No, and if he did, I'd turn him down." Nora precisely folded the dishtowel.

"Oh, you didn't have a good time? I'm surprised. Mac said he seemed like a nice guy. I was hoping… Oh, never mind." Beth hugged her. "I just want you to be happy."

"I *am* happy." And she had been until Harrison had come into her world and turned it upside down. Now she had to scramble to get her footing back. But her daughter didn't need to know any of that.

"You know what I mean."

Nora ignored the remark and straightened a stack of papers on the table.

"Okay, I get it. You don't want to talk about it." Beth rested a hand on the back of a kitchen chair.

Nora couldn't decide if Beth was going to sit

down, and she probably should ask her to, but she just wanted time alone.

Beth continued, "I heard that Dobbs is livid about the petition for the council to review their zoning decision."

"So I heard. Ran into him this morning and he didn't look pleased."

"Do you think you'll get enough signatures for them to reconsider?"

"It's not looking like we will."

"I'm sorry, Mom. Maybe Walt won't get that signature that rumor says he needs."

"Oh, I think he will." Nora moved around the table straightening the chairs.

"Why do you think that?"

Nora looked at Beth and sighed. "Because Harrison is Walt's cousin. He's in town to sign the papers."

"Oh, Mom." Beth came around the table and put her arms around her.

"I've tried everything I can think of to stop this from happening. I guess I'm just going to have to adjust to the reality."

"So Harrison told you he was Walt's cousin? That's why you won't go out with him again?"

"No, he omitted that detail. But we ran into Dobbs in town and the secret is out now."

Beth frowned. "Well, better you found out before things got serious between you two."

It would have been better if she'd known the truth from the beginning. If she'd known the truth before they went on a date. If she'd known the truth before he'd kissed her...

She decided it was time to change the subject. "So, I hear Sophie is coming to town this weekend with Chase to do a concert for the Autumn Arts Weekend."

"She is. I've missed her so much. I'm actually headed out to meet her this evening and Mac is watching the boys."

"I didn't think she'd miss an Autumn Arts Weekend since she basically ran them each year."

"She did her best to run things long distance this year. And Hunt and Keely helped out a lot. Between them helping at her gallery and helping with the festival, I'm not sure what she would have done without them."

"I heard they might buy a cabin here. They said they'd still return to Comfort Crossing soon, but they'd vacation at the cabin here plus come back so Hunt can continue working on his photography project."

"Sophie will be sorry to see them leave, but

at least she has Melissa to run the gallery when she's out on the road with Chase. She said they were going to try to cut back a bit on the traveling for a while. She sounded tired the last few times I talked to her."

"I heard one of Sophie and Chase's new songs playing on the radio this morning."

"Who knew my best friend would become a famous country singer?" Beth grinned. "Good thing she still talks to the little folk like me."

"As if Sophie would ever think she was better than anyone else. She's the most down-to-earth person I've met."

"Well, I can't wait to see her and catch up on everything."

"I'm sure I'll see her at the festival this weekend."

"She got tickets for all of us for the concert. Front row. Do you want to meet us there? Or we could pick you up."

"I'll meet you in town. Maybe half an hour before it starts?"

"Sounds good." Beth picked up her coat. "Well, I just wanted to check on you. I better run. Don't want to be late meeting Sophie."

"Tell her I said hi and I'll see her this weekend."

"Will do." Beth walked out the door, and Nora was strangely comforted by the twist their conversation had taken. Just normal talk. Familiar talk about Beth's best friend and one of Sweet River Falls' many festivals.

Normal.

Maybe her life could get back to just simple, familiar normal.

AFTER BETH LEFT, Nora decided that the windows *did* need cleaning. She got the window cleaner and a cloth and started to work. Outside windows first. Maybe some fresh air would do her good. Though she doubted it.

She turned as she heard a car pull up to the cabin. Annie, of course.

"You wouldn't pick up." Annie crossed the distance and climbed onto the porch, lounging against the railing.

"Sorry. I should have. That was rude."

"I just wanted to make sure you're okay."

"I'm fine. Just feeling a bit like a fool."

"You're not a fool."

"Annie, he was just spending time with me to get information about the lake and the area.

He's here to sell his portion. I'm a fool for thinking I had any feelings for him. He was just *using* me." She scrubbed at an imaginary spot on the window.

"I repeat, you're not a fool. *He's* a cad."

"Well, I *am* foolish. Here I was feeling all guilty about feelings for Harrison mixed up with my feelings for Ronnie and all that angst for nothing."

"You know what you need?"

"What?"

"A nice glass of wine with your best friend." Annie walked over and took the window cleaner out of her hand.

"I should go help with the dinner rush."

"You'll call over and say you're not coming over tonight. They can handle it without you."

"But… Nick will be expecting you at home."

"I already called him and told him I'll be late. Don't argue with me. You know I'll win."

Nora gave her a weak smile. "You always do."

They entwined their arms and walked into the cabin, Nora grateful for the support of her friend, as always.

∾

LINDA SAT on the porch of her cabin, going through the file she'd brought with her. Reading document after document. So much had changed in her life with the reading of those pages. She wasn't certain what she was going to do now.

Except stay away from that cabin across the lake. She didn't need Harrison to go and call the police on her.

She had enough problems right now. Enough complications in her life. Everything she'd been certain was a truth in her life had turned out to be lies. So many lies.

The now-familiar wave of sadness washed over her. She missed her parents, and it was always a dull ache in her soul now.

But she was also so very *angry* at them.

And they weren't here for her to yell at or for them to explain.

She looked down at the documents, almost ready to crumple them into a ball and throw them away.

But that would not erase the truth…

She looked across the distance and saw Harrison walking beside the lake. She grabbed the papers and slipped into the cabin before he could spy her. No use bringing more trouble her way.

"Sophie, you look exhausted." Beth still held her friend in a tight hug.

Sophie pulled away. "I'm okay. It's just tiring being on the road all the time. Different hotel every night. Planes. Trains. Buses. It takes some time to get used to it, I guess."

Beth frowned looking at the dark circles under Sophie's eyes. "You've lost weight. Too much."

"I'm fine. Don't worry about me. And Chase says we're going to cut back. We're actually planning on being back here for Christmas. I can't wait to be in Sweet River Falls for the holidays."

"Well, that will be great." Beth hugged her again. "Now, come on. We're going to Antonio's, and we're going to eat way too much and catch up on everything."

They walked arm and arm to their favorite restaurant, and Antonio enveloped Sophie in a hug as soon as he saw them. "There you are, my favorite famous singer. We've missed you."

"Cut it out." Sophie grinned as she hugged him back.

"I have your favorite table. Come on. Dinner is on me tonight."

They ordered margaritas and settled into the booth.

"So what's new with Mac and you?" Sophie slipped off her leather jacket—one Beth hadn't seen before—and dropped it onto the seat beside her. She had on designer jeans and some obviously new red cowboy boots. Of course, her friend would have new expensive clothes now. She was famous.

Beth looked down at her years-old golden-yellow sweater and jeans. Her own favorite cowboy boots poked out, in need of a good cleaning. She comforted herself with the fact that Mac had told her he loved that sweater on her and that it brought out the sparkles in her eyes.

"Beth?"

"Oh, yes. Mac and I are doing great. We're all adjusting to living together. The boys adore him. I'm surprised he hasn't been overwhelmed with all the changes, but he takes the boys and their constant energy and noise in stride."

"Well, you look happy." Sophie nodded approvingly.

"So do you. Just tired."

"I am happy. It's wonderful singing with Chase. When I'm on the stage I almost forget about how exhausting it is to get to that moment." She shrugged. "But I wouldn't give it up. Wouldn't give up Chase. It's just been a big change."

"I'll say. From running the gallery to country singer. You get the award for biggest change for the year."

"I don't know. You became a married woman." Sophie raised an eyebrow.

She smiled. "That I did."

"I'm glad you came back for Autumn Arts Weekend concert."

"Wouldn't miss it. *Couldn't* miss it. It's just such a big part of me."

"Well, I'm glad it is, because I miss you."

"I miss you too. FaceTime and Skyping aren't the same as seeing you in person."

The server brought their margaritas, and they began to talk as if they'd just spoken yesterday. Always in sync. Always starting up just where they'd left off the last time.

She'd missed Sophie so much while her

friend had been on the road this year, but she was so happy for her. Sophie was so vibrant and alive when she was singing. And it was obvious that Chase adored her.

Ah, but she did miss having Sophie around all the time.

She raised her glass. "To best friends forever."

"Forever," Sophie echoed.

CHAPTER 17

Harrison pulled his car into the driveway at his grandfather's cabin. He was determined to use this evening to feel out Walt and see if he could figure out what his cousin was up to. Somehow, he knew deep in his bones that Walt was not giving his mother a fair deal or telling the whole truth.

He crossed to the front door and knocked. Seemed strange to knock after so many times of just bursting through that door and into the hug from his grandmother when she'd still been alive. He was young when she died, but he still remembered her. After that, it had been the firm handshake of his grandfather greeting him. His grandfather had kept up the tradition of inviting him to the cabin every summer even after his grandmother died. Harrison thought his grandfather even began to look forward to it each year. The man had been so lonely after his wife died.

The door swung open, pulling him from his thoughts.

"Come in, come in." Walt swung his arm wide, motioning Harrison to come inside as if Walt owned the place.

That in and of itself got under Harrison's skin. He walked inside and swept his glance over the familiar room. He swallowed as memories assaulted him. Not much had changed, and a wave of nostalgia engulfed him. He steadied himself against the rush of emotions. His grandmother, his grandfather, his mother. So many good memories.

He turned to look at Walt.

And some very bad ones, too.

"Come on in. Here, what would you like to drink?" Walt walked over to the bar.

"Got a beer?"

"Sure." Walt opened a mini-fridge under the bar. "Take your pick."

He grabbed a bottle, twisted off the cap, and

took a swig. Walt made himself a bourbon on the rocks.

He glanced over to his grandfather's study. The door was closed, so he got no glimpse of his grandfather's beloved sanctuary.

"Sit down. Catch me up on your life." Walt was being more friendly to him than he'd ever been, acting like nothing had happened to blow their tenuous cousin relationship apart all those years ago. And it hadn't been *that* good to start with.

Walt lumbered over to the couch and sank down into the cushions. His cousin had lost his hard football player body and even struggled a bit for breath as he walked around. Such a role reversal from the jock Walt had been and the pudgy nerd Harrison had been.

Harrison took the seat across from Walt so he could watch his face while they talked.

"So, what brings you to town? I assume Aunt Ellen sent you with the papers? She could have done it all electronically, you know."

"I do know." Harrison took another swig of beer, eyeing Walt.

"It's a fair deal, don't you think? Now that she's in that retirement place, I'm sure you'd like a nice chunk of money to help pay for everything."

So Walt had been keeping up with how his mother was doing or at least where she was now. He decided to just not answer Walt's question but ask one of his own. "So, how long have you been living at the cabin?"

"Moved in after Grandfather died. Didn't want the place to go empty and get all tired looking. I was the only one around to take care of it. It's been my responsibility, all alone, all this time. I've been taking care of it, using my own money."

Harrison looked around the place. Everything looked exactly the same as it had the last time he'd been here, only older and more worn out. He'd noticed the roof was in need of repair as he pulled up. And did Walt think he hadn't looked at the trust financials? He knew darn well that Walt had turned in every repair bill for the trust to pay.

So, twenty years or so. Living rent-free in a paid-off house. Nice deal.

"I really do need Aunt Ellen to sign those papers. I'd hate to lose out. We've got a really good deal with this buyer. Who knows when someone else might come along. Cash deal. Really nice."

"So, are they going to renovate the cabin?"

"Oh, sure. I'm sure they will. Update it a bit."

Harrison pinned his lying cousin with a look. "Really? Then what's this I heard about you getting this land rezoned for condos?"

Walt's face turned red. "Well, that's just in case, you know. Wanted us to have lots of options for the sale."

"So, the buyer isn't going to put up condos here?"

"Well, I can't control what a buyer does, now can I?" Walt blustered.

"Walt, do you even know how to tell the truth?" He set his empty beer bottle on the table beside him.

"What do you mean?" Walt's face flushed an even brighter shade of red.

"You never seem to have a problem with lying to people. Even your family."

"If you're talking about that misunderstanding all those years ago…" Walt slurped a sip of his drink, the ice cubes rattling in the glass.

"It wasn't a *misunderstanding*. You lied."

"Well, you didn't live here full time like I did. I would have been thrown out of school. Lost my scholarship to college."

"If you'd told the truth and admitted what you did?" Harrison narrowed his eyes.

"Well, you were leaving soon anyway, and I figured it would all blow over by the next summer."

"Ah, but it didn't, did it?"

"How was I supposed to know that it wouldn't just... work out?"

"And it never occurred to you to tell Grandfather the truth?"

Walt set his drink down. "I don't know why you're bringing up ancient history. It doesn't really matter anymore, now does it? We were just kids."

"It pretty much ruined the relationship between my mother and Grandfather. You know she rarely came back after that... and I've *never* returned."

"Figured you were just busy with your life and didn't have time for a small town like Sweet River Falls."

He'd had enough of Walt's lies. "I should be getting back to the lodge."

"So you'll talk to your mother? We really should get this deal wrapped up."

"I'll talk to her." And he would. But he'd tell her exactly what was going on here. He didn't trust Walt one little bit. The man had not changed.

"Well, come back by anytime." Walt said it as if he had the right to invite Harrison to the cabin. That cabin that was by all rights half Harrison's... well, half his mother's.

Harrison stood, gritting his teeth against the anger surging through him.

"Talk to Aunt Ellen." His cousin's demanding tone only served to fuel his anger.

Harrison turned and walked out of the cabin and into the cool night, dragging in deep breaths of the pine-scented air, trying to calm his jangled nerves and tangled emotions. He harbored such resentment toward Walt from when they'd been boys. After what he'd done. Was that clouding his judgment now?

No, he didn't think so.

He drove slowly back to the lodge and parked his car in front of the cabin. But instead of going inside, he walked to the lake and climbed up on the rock overlooking the lake. Nora's favorite rock.

As mad as he was at Walt for lying to him, he knew Nora now felt the same way about him. He *had* lied to her. It was a lie of omission, and it had been to protect his mother's interests, but still. He needed to try to make things right with her.

If she'd ever speak to him again…

CHAPTER 18

Harrison walked out into the crisp morning air, determined to find Nora. He headed along the path by the lake. A lone blue heron waded at the water's edge. It paused and stood looking at him as if sizing him up. He smiled at the bird and waved, as silly as that was. The bird took another long look at him, then a few gangly steps, and it took off and flew across the lake.

He continued along the path and ran into Mac at a bench beside the lake.

"Harrison." Mac's voice was no longer friendly and welcoming.

"Morning, Mac." He kept his voice deliberately friendly and cheerful. "Beautiful day, huh?"

"Uh-huh."

"I'm looking for Nora."

"She doesn't want to see you." Mac stood and faced him. "I won't have you hurting her. Beth's mom means the world to me."

"I didn't mean to hurt her. I was actually headed to talk to her and explain everything when we ran into Walt."

Mac eyed him with an unbelieving look.

Harrison sighed. "I was trying to keep my real identity a secret while I tried to figure out what Walt was up to. You see, my mom owns half-interest in the property. I was checking things out for her. I was afraid if Walt knew I was in town, he might cover his tracks. I think he's trying to swindle my mom."

Mac frowned. "Your mom owns half the property?"

"Yes, and Walt sent her sale papers to sign, but... well, something's not right. But then I've never been one to trust Walt."

"You got that part right." Mac nodded.

"So I wasn't exactly trying to keep secrets from Nora. I just... I didn't want anyone to know. I had to put my mom's interests first. But then when Nora and I—well, as we got closer, I knew I should tell her who I was.

Explain why I hadn't told her Walt was my cousin."

"But you're here to get those papers signed. You're just trying to get your mother a fairer deal?" Mac's eyes narrowed.

"Now that I've been back here... I'm not sure Walt's making the right decision. And if indeed the property is going to a condo complex, I don't think my mother *will* sign. Anyway, I was here trying to find out things regarding the sale. Had my Mom's best interest at heart, but I sure didn't mean to hurt Nora in the process. I didn't want Walt to know I was in town until I was ready to confront him. But it all kind of backfired with Nora. I screwed up."

Mac rubbed his chin. "Then, I expect you should go over and find Nora and explain that to her. She's in the kitchen at the dining hall."

Harrison nodded and hurried off to find Nora, hopeful that she'd give him a chance to explain.

Nora looked up from where she was scrubbing a pot to see Harrison standing in the doorway to the kitchen. He crossed the distance with determined strides. She turned her back on him and returned to scrubbing the pot even though it was spotless now.

"Nora, can we talk?"

"Nothing to say. And I'm busy now." She kept her back to him.

He stepped beside her and touched her arm. "Please. Give me just a couple of minutes."

She ignored the heat flooding through her from his touch. She ignored the urgency in his voice. And she absolutely refused to look at his eyes. They were always her downfall.

"As I said, I'm busy."

"Hey, Nora." She turned at the sound of Mac's voice, grateful for an excuse to avoid Harrison.

"Morning, Mac."

Her son-in-law crossed over to stand beside her. "It's none of my business, and I should really stay out of it, but I think you should at least hear what Harrison has to say."

Mac was right, it wasn't his business.

"I'll finish scrubbing those pots. Give the man five minutes of your time. Please?"

She set the pot down in the soapy water, still avoiding looking at Harrison. "Five minutes." She turned and walked out the back door to the kitchen, glancing at her watch, determined to give him exactly five minutes. Not a second more.

She continued down to the lake and stood on the shoreline. Harrison came to stand beside her.

"First, I want to apologize. I didn't mean for you to get hurt."

She still didn't look at him.

"I was just here trying to figure out what Walt was up to before he could find out I was in town. I think... actually, I'm fairly certain he's trying to swindle my mother with the sale of the family property."

She frowned. "Your mother?"

"She owns half the property, but she isn't really up to dealing with all of this right now. She's been ill. Recovering from pneumonia. And, honestly, I don't trust Walt to be giving her a fair deal."

She remained quiet, letting him continue. His mother. He'd been doing this for his mother.

"Anyway, I've talked to the estate lawyer. There's a missing will, and I can't find out any information on the trust that's put in an offer on the land. I was afraid if Walt knew I was in town, he'd make it even harder to find out the truth, not that I've had much luck." Harrison let out a long sigh. "But once you and I got close... after I... after I kissed you, I knew I needed to tell you the truth. I was coming to find you when we ran into Walt. Good old Walt. Always messing with my life. But that's no excuse. I should have told you when we were at Harmony Haven Inn. But I kind of just got wrapped up in the moment. My feelings—"

He stopped then and looked out at the lake. "I should have told you before I kissed you. It wasn't fair to you. You should have known who I was. I'm sorry. I didn't set out to trick you, I was just trying to protect my mom."

He turned to her, and she finally looked into his eyes. His eyes held regret, sincerity... and did they show desire?

"Could we start again? Please? With no more secrets?" He reached out his hand.

She stood there looking into those eyes of his, resisting. She turned to look at the lake, ignoring his outstretched hand. She let the lake calm her, soothe her. She finally answered him. "I understand why you did it. To protect your mom. But I just can't get over the fact you lied to me. I feel like you used me. Tricked me to get information."

"It wasn't like that. Honestly, I'm so sorry you were hurt. I wish I could have handled it differently. I should have told you after I got to know you. I know you would have understood and kept my secret."

Emotions warred through her. So many emotions. It was hard to stand firm against a man who was just trying to protect his mother.

She turned to look at him again. "I realize that now, but I just don't think I can… we can… well, I don't think I can go out with you again. There's really no starting over. What we had, whatever it was… I just… can't." And really, it would be easier this way. She wouldn't have to sort out her feelings for Harrison or the guilt she had regarding Ronnie.

She just needed a simple life. Craved it. She wanted her old, uncomplicated life back.

He reached out again and took her hand in his and squeezed it. The connection jolted her, and heat rushed through her. Part of her wanted to grab onto that hand and hold on. But her practical side won, and she withdrew her hand.

"I'm really sorry, Nora." He looked at her

with his piercing blue eyes, and it took her breath away.

He turned and slowly walked away. She stood there fighting her emotions, trying to find her balance.

The thought flashed through her mind that she should run after him and forgive him and give them another chance. The *ridiculous* thought. She turned to the lake, hoping it would weave its magic and soothe her soul.

Mac walked up to where Beth stood at the sink, doing the dinner dishes. "I've got the boys all settled down in their rooms. Told them they had twenty minutes to read and I'd be back in to turn out the lights."

His strong arms encircled her waist, and she leaned back against him, ever grateful for his love *and* his help with the boys. "Thanks. They seem to really listen to you."

He pressed a kiss on her neck. "Yep, except when they don't."

She turned around in his arms and hugged him. "You know, I think I'm one of the luckiest women on the planet."

"Just one of them?" he teased.

"Okay, *the* luckiest. Seriously, I love you. I can't imagine our lives without you."

He kissed her gently on the lips. "Nor can I imagine mine without the three of you. And your mom and brother and Bree and Cece. Well, my whole extended family now. Never thought I'd have that."

She turned back to do the dishes, and he grabbed a dishtowel. "So, I ran into Harrison at the lodge today."

She looked up at him. "I figured he'd move to a different place to stay while he's in town. Did you ask him to leave?"

"No, he actually talked to me for a bit. Explained why he hadn't told people he was Dobbs's cousin."

"What lame excuse did he give?" She was still furious her mother had gotten hurt. She was pretty certain her mom had started to have feelings for the man.

"He didn't want Walt to know he was in town. He doesn't trust him."

"That's smart at least."

"He was trying to protect his mother's interest in the property." He explained what Harrison had told him.

She handed him the plate she'd just washed. "So he was just helping his mom out?"

"Appears so."

"So he needs to explain this to Mom."

"Exactly what I told him."

"But I bet Mom won't listen to him. She's stubborn."

Mac grinned. "So is her daughter. But I went and asked her to give him a chance to explain. Now it's up to her to forgive him and decide what she wants to do about her relationship with him."

"I think she likes him."

"Maybe. Yeah, I think so too. But it's up to her how things work out from here."

Mac was right. It was up to her Mom from here. She just hoped that her mother would give Harrison a chance. She wanted to see her mom happy. To have someone in her life again who cared for her. Maybe Harrison could be that person.

If her mother would give him another chance.

CHAPTER 19

H arrison got up early the next morning and sat beside the pathway that Nora took each morning to get to the dining hall. He knew she'd said there was no chance for them, but he couldn't get her out of his mind. Maybe they could just be some kind of friends? That was probably the best he could hope for. At the very least, he could try to ease the tension between them.

Nora walked into view. She paused when she saw him sitting on the rock. He held his breath, wondering if she would turn around and go back the other way. After a moment, she continued toward him.

"Morning," he greeted her tentatively.

"Morning."

Not cold, not warm. Just neutral. Well, that was a start.

"I thought I might catch breakfast at the dining hall this morning. Now that I've run into you, mind if I walk the rest of the way with you?" Ran into her. As if. He'd been sitting out here for forty-five minutes, not sure what time she went to the lodge.

"Sure." Once again, not enthusiastic, but not totally dismissive either.

They headed along the pathway beside the lake. Nora paused, and he stopped to see what she was looking at. A lone blue heron stood by the lake, looking at them. He swore he saw a tiny frown cross Nora's face. They walked past the heron, and Nora looked back over her shoulder at it before heading on down the path.

"Nice day out." He thought he'd try some safe small talk.

"It is. I heard we might have some snowfall coming next week."

"Really? It's been so mild so far."

"Colorado is like that. Nice one day, snow the next."

They continued on in silence. He finally made small talk again. "Thought I might try the pecan pancakes this morning."

"Always a good choice."

"Think you could join me?" He was at least going to try.

"I've got a busy day." She climbed the steps to the lodge. "Enjoy your meal."

With that, she disappeared inside. He stood on the porch, looking out at the lake. His hunger finally propelled him inside for the promised pancakes.

NORA HID out in the kitchen, avoiding Harrison. She let the servers handle delivering all the orders and refills of coffee. She didn't check on their customers even once, and she felt guilty about it. But that's why she had employees, right? To help with the workload.

"You going to tell me what's going on?" Judy set a baking sheet of fresh cinnamon rolls on the counter beside her.

"Nothing's going on."

"You're always flitting in and out of the kitchen, checking on things. You haven't left the kitchen once this morning."

"I'm just trying to help you out more."

"Honestly, Nora, you know I adore you...

but your *help* this morning has been... well, not so helpful."

Nora looked down where she was cleaning up a mound of flour that she'd managed to spill all over the counter and floor. "I might be a bit distracted."

"Why don't you go out and have you a good big breakfast?"

That's the last thing she needed. "Not hungry." Her stomach chose that exact moment to growl loudly as if mocking her.

"Okay, then how about you go see if they need help at the reception desk. Or catch up on paperwork. I'll finish cleaning up this mess."

Nora sighed. She knew when Judy was ready to throw her out of her kitchen, and this was probably more than just a suggestion. There was no need to drag Judy into her mood or her problems.

She turned and almost went out the back door to the kitchen to circle around to another door to sneak into her office without being seen. But that was *ridiculous*. The man was not going to chase her away from her own dining room. She pushed through the door and entered the dining room, her gaze sweeping the room, looking for Harrison.

He spied her and their eyes met. His eyes. Those darn eyes of his. They had some magnetic pull, weaving a spell over her. She looked away. Then back at him. He lifted a hand in a wave.

She smiled and nodded. Just like she'd do toward any guest.

He pointed at the chair across from him as if asking her to join him again.

She stood in the doorway, torn with indecision. Her stomach growled again, taunting her.

Since when was she a weak, scared woman? Afraid to have a simple breakfast with a man? It didn't mean anything. It was just a meal. She took a deliberate step toward him, then paused again, undecided. With a brief shake of her head, wondering what she was doing, she continued to his table.

"Judy threw me out of her kitchen. That offer for joining you for breakfast still available?"

"Certainly." He jumped up and held the chair out for her.

She slipped into her chair and waved to a waitress. "I'll have the pecan pancakes and coffee."

"Yes, ma'am." The waitress hurried away.

"Go ahead and finish your breakfast." She motioned to his half-eaten plate of pancakes smothered in maple syrup with a big side order of bacon.

"I can wait for yours to come."

"Don't be silly. Finish it while it's hot."

"You're right that the pancakes are delicious."

Talking about food was safe, right? "They are."

The waitress brought her coffee, and Nora let it sit for a bit to cool off.

"Coffee is good, too." Harrison continued with the safe food conversation.

"Thanks. It's from a local coffee place. They roast their own beans." Safe. Safe. Safe.

She took a sip of the coffee which was still too hot to really drink so she set it back on the table, unfolded her napkin, and placed it in her lap. She straightened the salt and pepper shakers against the container that held sugar and sweetener on the table. Then she leaned over and moved the chair next to her so it was straight with the tabletop instead of at an angle.

Harrison shot her an amused look. "Does it help?"

"Does what help?"

"Moving all those things back into place. Does that make you feel more in control of your life?"

She looked at him in amazement. That wasn't what she was trying to do.

Was it?

She grinned sheepishly and shrugged. "Maybe? I don't like to feel out of control of things."

"I get that."

The server brought her breakfast, and she attacked the stack of pancakes. Something to concentrate on besides his eyes.

HARRISON WAS MORE than pleased Nora had joined him for breakfast. Surprised *and* pleased.

The conversation lagged between them while she ate her meal. He sipped his coffee and glanced around the room. That Linda woman sat by herself in the corner, but he'd swear he saw her making furtive glances at him all through the meal. He probably should have called the police when he found her at the cabin. There was something about her. Something mysterious. But he didn't need another mystery to unravel while he was here. He had enough just figuring out what Walt was up to.

"That was delicious." Nora pushed her plate away.

"I agree." He quit looking at Linda and brought his attention back to Nora.

She brushed a lock of hair from her eyes and reached for her coffee. They sat there sipping coffee and not talking.

But at least she was sitting here with him. And her eyes no longer shot flashes of anger at him.

Baby steps. He was okay with baby steps.

CHAPTER 20

T he next morning Harrison sat in his car, pulled off the side of a service road near his grandfather's cabin, and tucked back a ways so his car couldn't be seen. He'd been here over an hour, hoping Walt would leave. He drummed his fingers on the steering wheel and waited. Maybe Walt wasn't planning on leaving the cabin today. He waited some more.

He finally saw Walt drive past, headed toward town.

He turned on the car and drove to the cabin, once again parking in the clearing past the cabin, just in case Walt returned. He reminded himself that he had every right to be there, but still, a twinge of guilt passed through him as he climbed onto the porch. But he hadn't been able to find out any information on the company buying the property. They'd hidden their tracks well. He was certain that Walt was hiding the information, and he needed it so he could protect his mom.

He had every right to be here. He kept repeating that mantra. Besides, he'd do anything for his mom, including entering a cabin that she, by rights, co-owned.

He crossed the porch, and a small smile crossed his lips when he found a key to the cabin still hidden under an old oil can in the weathered cabinet at the end of the porch. So much had changed. Some things hadn't.

He went to the door, unlocked it, and stepped inside.

The absolute quiet surrounded him. He stood still, soaking in the smell, the surroundings, the memories. The pine ceiling rose high above the entrance. Light streamed in through the windows across the room on the lake side of the cabin.

He swallowed as he remembered the last time he'd been here with his grandfather. He'd been standing in front of those windows, facing his grandfather. His grandfather's voice had been strong and firm and so full of disappointment, commanding Harrison to leave.

He could feel the soul-crushing pain in his chest at those words. And he'd been unable to explain anything to his grandfather.

So he'd turned and walked out of the cabin all those years ago and never saw his grandfather again. And he'd never returned until this trip.

He chased away the painful memories before they could overwhelm him. But he was pulled, as if by magic, to the mantel full of photos. He picked up a wooden-framed photo of his grandmother, his grandfather, and him as a young boy. He was surprised that a photo of him had survived in the cabin. He set the photo down gingerly, and with one last melancholy glance at it, he turned and headed toward the study.

As expected, Walt had taken over the room. Papers were strewn across the old wooden desk. Harrison crossed the room and carefully riffled through the papers, trying not to move them from where Walt had put them.

An official-looking document caught his eye, and he grabbed it and crossed to the window to read it in the light. Articles of Organization for the Blue Horizon Company. He'd seen that before, but it only listed a registered agent, not who actually was part of the company. He shifted through more papers until he came to a list of private investors in the company.

Exactly what he'd been looking for.

He read through the papers and wasn't surprised to find Walt was actually an investor in the company. So was Chuck Smith, who owned Alpine Outfitters. No surprise they were still buddies. He read through the list of other investors, but no more names seemed familiar to him. He snapped some photos of the papers with his phone.

He walked back to the desk and set the papers back where he found them. On a table at the side of the room, there were plans spread out for a sprawling condo development.

He looked at some other pages resting on the table and frowned. It looked like Walt also would get a free penthouse condo for life to live in with the deal. He snapped a photo of that agreement, too.

Finally, he was getting to the bottom of everything.

Walt was up to his old tricks. Protecting his interests. He was selling the family property for a low price to a company he had an interest in. But he'd make his money back on condo sales, not to mention a free place to live.

He wondered if Walt had ever paid for a place to live in his whole life.

Anger surged through him. Walt was trying to trick his mother. Give her half of the low selling price, while he would get his money from condo sales and the growth of the company.

Well, it wasn't going to happen. He was going to stop his cousin dead in his tracks. Partially to protect his mother, but he couldn't help but admit it also was a bit of revenge for what Walt had done to him all those years ago.

And even after being away for all these years, he had to admit he didn't like the thought of the cabin being torn down. Gone forever.

Harrison took one last look around the study, hoping he'd gotten everything back in place, and left.

When he got back to his cabin at the lodge, he called his mother. She didn't pick up her cell, but that wasn't unusual. She rarely kept it with her in the retirement center. He called the reception desk at the center. Jolene, the receptionist, answered in her normal perky voice.

"Jolene. Harrison Stanworth. I'm looking for my mother."

"Oh, she just walked by a few minutes ago and was headed back to her room. Said she was going to rest for a bit. Do you want me to send someone to get her?"

"No, don't bother her. I'll just try her later." He hung up the phone. He was anxious to tell his mother everything that he'd found out now that he had proof. But she'd been tired since the pneumonia episode, so he'd let her rest and try again later. Maybe next time he called, by some miracle, she'd even have her cell phone with her.

CHAPTER 21

Nora saw Harrison sitting at his usual table by the window for breakfast the next morning. He was eating alone again. He hadn't joined Linda for a meal since that first night.

Not that it mattered to her one way or the other.

Torn between hiding in the kitchen and going to pour him some more coffee, the practical, businesswoman side won out. It was her job to see that her customers had hot coffee, right? That was all it was. Just doing her job.

She grabbed the coffeepot and headed toward his table.

A wide smile spread across his face as she approached. "Good morning, Nora." His deep, throaty voice wrapped around her and his clear blue eyes sparkled with welcome.

But she ignored the friendly tone of his voice *and* his smiling eyes and used her best just-doing-her-job voice. "Coffee?"

"Love some." He held out his cup.

She filled his cup and was annoyed to see a slight shake to her hand.

"Do you have time to join me for a cup?"

She glanced around the dining room. She couldn't use the excuse they were busy, because most of the tables were empty. "I… I suppose I could."

She walked over to the sidebar, got a cup for herself, and poured it full of coffee. She turned to walk back to his table and splashed some on the floor. She stopped, cleaned up her mess, and continued to the table, slipping into the chair across from him but making sure her legs didn't bump up against his legs stretched out under the table.

Not that she noticed his long legs so close to hers. In fact, there was *so much* about him that she just didn't notice. At all.

"Do you have a wedding here at the lodge this weekend?" Harrison shifted in his seat and his legs brushed hers.

She moved her legs farther away. "No, not this weekend. This weekend is the big Autumn Arts Weekend in town, so we decided to not book one at the same time. We get a lot of regulars who come to the lodge for the festival, year after year. Wanted the rooms available for them."

"So what's this arts festival about?"

"Well, most of the shops will be open and showcase arts and crafts from the area. Beth's best friend, Sophie, owns a gallery here. She'll have that open with displays. There's an Arts and Crafts Fair at the arena in town on Saturday. Lots of fun things and handcrafted items displayed there. Then, Sophie and Chase —Chase Green, the country singer—do you know him? Anyway, Sophie sings with Chase now, and they're giving a concert tonight."

Mac walked up to the table. "Hey, Nora, Harrison. You coming into town soon for the festival?"

"Nora was just telling me about it. That all sounds interesting. I guess I'll head into town and poke around."

"Nora, you should have him come with you. Show him around."

She glared at Mac, but he ignored it. Harrison looked at her expectantly.

"Do you want to come with me to the festival?" It would be rude not to invite him after Mac had suggested it.

"I'd love to." He said it so quickly she had no time to come up with an excuse to withdraw the invitation or why it was a bad idea.

But it was just the friendly thing to do. Show a stranger around town. Then she frowned. But he wasn't a stranger. He'd been to Sweet River Falls before. His family owned half the Dobbs place.

"Well, Beth and I and the boys will see you in town later, then." Mac headed out of the dining room. Traitor. Why had he insisted she invite Harrison?

Well, he hadn't *insisted*. Just suggested. And she'd jumped right in to invite him. Her forehead crinkled.

"You changing your mind on the invite?" He cocked his head to one side, staring at her.

"No." But she kind of wished she could. She took a sip of her coffee. "I'm planning on going after the noon meal here in the dining room. Leave here about one-thirty."

"I'll just meet you here, then?"

"Sure."

Harrison stood. "Well, I have some work I need to get done before we head into town." He turned and walked away.

She sat and finished her coffee, staring out the window at the lake. She didn't want to have Harrison come with her to the festival. And yet... she did. How come being with Harrison felt like she was on an icy road at the top of a mountain with her car teetering on the edge?

NORA CLIMBED out of Harrison's sports car with as much grace as she could manage. He'd held her hand firmly in his and pulled her out of the low-slung seat. She stood and tried to look nonchalant. Everything was going to be okay. She was just showing him around the festival.

They walked from the parking area to Main Street, which had been blocked off to car traffic. People wandered through vendors set up on the street and in and out of the shops lining the street.

"Wow, there's a lot of people here." Harrison glanced around at the crowds.

"The festival does bring a lot of tourists to

town. It's good for business. It's one of our more popular festivals."

He eyed her. "Do you have a lot of festivals?"

She grinned. "We do. In the summer we have one almost every weekend. Some bigger than others, of course. The May Festival that officially opens tourist season and the Autumn Arts Weekend are probably the biggest."

"I see."

"Oh, come on. I see Sophie standing outside her gallery." She headed through the crowd toward Brooks Gallery with Harrison following behind her. Or she figured he was. She didn't look back to check on him, afraid she'd run into those eyes of his. Or his warm smile. Or he'd find some reason to take her hand in his again like when she'd gotten out of his car…

HARRISON HURRIED AFTER NORA, wishing he'd thought to grab her hand so he didn't lose her in the crowd. Or he'd thought to grab her hand just so he could hold it in his…

He walked up to where Nora had her arms

wrapped around a young woman. They were both laughing and talking at once.

Nora pulled away, still holding the woman's hand.

Lucky woman…

"This is Sophie Brooks, Beth's best friend, and my almost-daughter."

"Hi, nice to meet you, Sophie."

"Nice to meet you. Why don't you both come into the gallery? Hunt has a fabulous new photography exhibit up."

They walked into the gallery, where Sophie introduced him to Hunt Robichaux, the photographer, and his wife, Keely. Then he met a Melissa who he thought helped run the gallery. He struggled to keep the names straight.

"And this is Chase." Sophie beamed as she introduced him. Chase wrapped an arm around her waist.

"Nice to meet you, Chase."

Just then Mac and the boys came into the gallery. "Boys, best behavior. This is Miss Sophie's gallery, not a place to goof around."

"Trevor, Connor." Sophie opened her arms wide and hugged the boys, kissing on them.

"Yuck, Miss Sophie." Connor swiped his face as if to wipe off the kisses.

"I haven't seen you two in forever."

"That's 'cause Mom says you're on the road all the time. Why are you on the road? Do you just go out and sit on them or something? I'm not allowed on the road without my mom," Trevor added seriously.

"It's an expression, kiddo. It means she's out of town." Mac ruffled the boy's hair.

"Oh." He turned to Sophie. "Miss Sophie, Mom said you're singing tonight and we get to stay up late and go to your concert. But we have to be on our best behavior."

"I'm glad you're coming." Sophie turned to Harrison. "We've got an extra ticket to the show tonight if you'd like to come."

He didn't miss the slightly panicked look on Nora's face. "I'd love to."

"Great." Sophie smiled.

Nora didn't.

Harrison did. A big wide grin.

The day was getting better and better as far as he was concerned.

CHAPTER 22

They walked out of the gallery, and Mac took the boys off to ride some of the rides at the end of the street while Harrison tried to sort through all the names he'd heard and who was who.

Nora was looking at the food vendors lining the street.

"You want something?" he asked.

"A funnel cake?" Her eyes lit up like a kid's at Christmas.

"Why not? My diet's been shot since I got to town."

They got the funnel cake and wandered down to a courtyard area and sat on the brick wall while they ate the delicious treat.

"You got some powdered sugar..." He reached out and gently dabbed at the side of her mouth.

She licked her lips. "Ah, thanks."

He stared at her mouth while trying to tell himself not to. He broke off another bite of the funnel cake to distract himself. "Haven't had one of these since I was a kid. I forgot how great they are." He patted his stomach. "Seriously going on a diet when I get back to Chicago."

And suddenly he was in no hurry to get back. He'd forgotten how much he loved this little town. The friendly people. The fresh Colorado air.

And now there was Nora.

Chicago was so far away from Sweet River Falls. So far from Nora.

Nora took the last bite of their treat, and he got up and threw away their trash. He returned to sit beside her. His hand brushed against hers resting on the edge of the wall. But not on purpose, of course.

Now that they were sitting and resting, he wanted to talk to her about what he'd found at his grandfather's cabin and get her take on things. He cleared his throat. "So, I was wondering if I could run something past you. Get your opinion."

"Of course."

"So... I happened to run across some information—"

Before he could finish, a woman came hurrying up to them, her eyes flashing. "Nora Cassidy, will you ever stop causing trouble?"

"Hello, Gloria."

He didn't miss that Nora's voice didn't have its normal friendly tone to it.

"Why are you trying to cause all these problems for Walter? All he wants to do is sell his land." The woman—Gloria—stood with her hands on her hips.

Walt's land. Interesting choice of words. Harrison stayed silent and watched the exchange between the two women.

"That petition is just preposterous. The zoning committee already ruled. Why do you always insist on stirring things up?"

"Because I believe the zoning shouldn't have changed. I think Lone Elk Lake should stay like it is. It's peaceful and beautiful." Nora's words were firm and strong.

"You're standing in the way of progress.

Always so backward with your rustic, run-down lodge. Have you ever thought of selling it? I bet more condos would be a great addition there, too. Bring more people into town."

Harrison looked at the woman who'd just slammed Nora's pride and joy. Before he could defend her, Nora stood and faced the woman. "No, I have *not* thought of selling the lodge. And it's not run-down. But you know that."

The Gloria woman seemed to finally notice he was sitting there. "Oh, I'm sorry. It looks like Nora isn't going to introduce you. So rude. I'm Gloria Edmonds."

"Harrison Stanworth."

A look of recognition flashed across her face. "Walter's cousin? So nice to meet you. Walter has gotten you such a great deal on the sale of the property. So I heard."

Or so Walt wanted everyone to think what a swell guy he was.

"You must be glad that he could do that for you. Take care of the details, I mean." Gloria smiled at him.

Nora narrowed her eyes, looking at Gloria closely. "How come you know so much about it?"

"Well, Walter and I are friends, of course. Always looking out for what's in the best interest of the town."

Nora laughed but didn't say anything.

Gloria Edmonds. Why did he know that name?

"Nora, I don't see why you'd want to oppose this and ruin Mr. Stanworth's chance for a good sale."

Gloria turned to him and switched on the charm. Her eyes flickered, and a coy smile crossed her lips. "Well, Mr. Stanworth, I'd be glad to show you around the festival if you'd like. I'm sure Nora has to hurry back to her little lodge. She's such a little worker bee, you know."

He was pretty sure he'd never heard a more condescending tone of voice. "Nope, Nora and I are having a great time." He stood up and rested his hand on Nora's arm. She didn't pull away, which surprised him.

"Well, if you change your mind, or if you'd like to be shown around to the… well, *nicer* areas of town, you just call me." She pressed a card into his hand. "Well, I should go. They asked me to judge the quilt contest, but I already know who will win." She winked, then turned and hurried away.

"Wow… who was *that?*"

"*That* was Gloria Edmonds. And I'm sure she's decided one of her friends will win the first prize at the quilt contest without so much as looking at all the entries."

"I don't think she likes you much." He gave Nora a wry grin.

"Nope, not since the second grade."

"Well, that's a long time. What happened in the second grade?"

"It's kind of a long story…"

"I've got time." He settled back on the wall and she sat beside him.

"So, one day in second grade Annie came to school with her hair in braids. She was so proud of them because her father had done them for her. Her mother had died the year before, and her father was doing his best to raise her. Okay, the braids *were* crooked, but he'd tried. Gloria started calling Annie Crooked Braids from then on. Annie never wore braids again. After about two days of her taunting Annie, I'd had enough. I stood up to Gloria— which no one ever did—and told her to back off."

"And did she?"

"Well, mostly."

"So, this is all about braids and name-calling?"

Nora rolled her eyes. "Nope. Then a few days later we were taking a test. I sat next to Gloria. Not my choice, the teacher picked the seating chart. Anyway, Gloria was acting weird and turning away from me. I ignored her and worked on the test. Still remember it. A spelling test. Anyway, Gloria raised her hand and said I was copying off of her. I, of course, insisted I wasn't. Gloria's friend sitting beside her said she'd seen me copying off of Gloria, too. The teacher made me bring my paper to the front, gave me a zero. I was mortified."

"The teacher wouldn't listen to you?"

"It was two against one, I guess. And the teacher—Mrs. Ridley—will never forget her name—she made me sit on the bench at recess that day instead of play." Nora frowned. "I was so astonished she wouldn't believe me. Anyway, Annie came over and sat beside on the bench and said she believed me. We've been best friends ever since."

"So something good came out of it."

"Yes. Then I went on to beat Gloria in the spelling bee championship that year. It's the little things, you know?" Nora grinned.

He laughed. "And after all these years, *that* makes her not like you?"

"Oh, no. That was just the start." Nora shook her head. "Lots of things. Annie had a sweater her mother had knitted her before she died. She loved that sweater so much. Gloria spilled paint on it. On purpose, of course, but claimed it was an accident. Then smirked after the teacher turned away."

"The same Mrs. Ridley?"

"The very same. Turns out Mrs. Ridley and Gloria's mother were friends, so Gloria was always believed."

"Sounds like grade school was brutal."

"Nah, I had Annie. She had me. Then... there was high school. If Annie or I were interested in a boy, Gloria would set her sights on him. She fought us on getting the riverwalk put in along Sweet River behind the shops, too. I think she just fought it because Annie and I spearheaded the effort. There's more, but let's just say it's been going on for years. I mostly try to ignore her."

"She appears to be the kind of person who's hard to ignore."

Nora sighed. "Don't I know it."

He really wanted to hear the whole long

complete story of Gloria Edmonds, but he could tell Nora wanted to drop it. "So, how about we wander around town some more?"

Nora nodded in approval. "Yes, let's. But how about we avoid the quilt judging?"

He grinned at her. "Sounds like a plan."

CHAPTER 23

Nora almost hated to admit to herself what a good time she was having with Harrison at the festival. They'd continued walking around town, grabbed a bite to eat, and talked. Always talking. He told her about his job and how his mother had recently moved into a retirement facility. She had her own apartment there and a handful of her friends were there, too. Nora liked that he seemed so involved in his mother's life and making sure she was well taken care of and happy.

And protected her best interests, which had started the whole problems between Harrison and her...

They talked about Connor and Trevor and all the sports they played. She talked about the lodge and the recent improvements they'd been able to do.

Before she knew it, it was time to head over for Sophie and Chase's concert. He took hold of her elbow as they crossed the rocky parking area and headed to the small arena. As they entered the building, she realized he never had talked to her about whatever he'd started into before Gloria interrupted them.

She showed their tickets to the ticket taker, and they made their way to the front row.

"Grams!" Connor waved wildly. "Over here."

They walked up to the front.

"We're in the very first row." Trevor practically bounced in his seat next to Beth and Mac.

"Trevor, I know you're excited, but settle down." Beth put her hand on the boy's leg.

They took their seats, and Nora looked around at the crowd. The seats were filling up rapidly. She'd heard the concert was sold out. No surprise there. Not only was Chase a big name in country music, Sweet River Falls was proud of their hometown girl who'd made it big in the industry, too.

Soon the lights flooded the stage and Sophie

and Chase walked out. The crowd rose to their feet, clapping.

Nora smiled. Sophie looked so happy, and it was hard to miss the look in Chase's eyes when he glanced at her. Sophie deserved this happiness in her life.

The duo started singing what had become their signature song—Road to Forgiveness. They sang song after song, each one ending in a round of applause.

Chase stepped forward. "Now, if you don't mind me singing a solo…" He waved to a stagehand, who brought a stool for Sophie. "Here, sit. I have a surprise for you."

Sophie smiled at him and took the stool. He strummed his guitar and turned to Sophie. "This is one I wrote for you."

He sang a beautiful melody of forgiveness and finding one's true love. He got closer to Sophie as he started the last verse.

"And sometimes you meet the perfect person at the most unexpected time. Their heart beats in sync with you and completes you. If you're lucky enough to find that person, don't let them go."

The music drifted away, and he set his guitar down and dropped to one knee. The arena went silent as if everyone was holding their breath.

"Sophie. You are that person for me. You are part of me. I love you... will you marry me?" He held out a ring box.

Sophie jumped up, tears rolling down her cheeks. Chase stood, and Sophie threw her arms around his neck. "Of course I will. You're my perfect person, too."

They kissed, and the crowd went wild. Nora glanced over at Beth and saw tears streaming down her face. Beth glanced over at her and smiled.

So much happiness and joy. Nora's heart swelled. Sophie was like a daughter to her, and she couldn't be happier for her.

"You okay?" Harrison leaned close to her ear.

"Yes, why?"

"Well, you're... crying."

Nora realized she had tears on her own cheeks, and she smiled. "I couldn't be better."

BETH ENTERED THE BACKSTAGE AREA, searching for Sophie. She was surrounded by people, with

Chase right by her side. Sophie looked up, saw her, and waved. She stood on tiptoe to say something to Chase, then hurried over.

Beth threw her arms around her friend. "Oh, Sophie. I'm so happy for you."

Sophie grinned. "I'm kinda happy for me, too. I had no idea."

"And that song he wrote for you. It was so beautiful."

"Don't make me start crying again," Sophie threatened with a smile. "I don't know how I got so lucky."

"Maybe because you deserve it?" Beth hugged her again.

Chase threaded his way through the crowd, stopping to say something to a few people before he finally came up to them. He slipped his arm around Sophie. "I guess I surprised her, huh?"

Beth laughed. "I guess you surprised everyone."

"Thank goodness she said yes. That would have been quite a mess, wouldn't it?" He tossed Sophie a lazy grin.

"Well, you're lucky that I said yes, I guess, then." Sophie leaned against him.

"Well, I have to go rescue Mac. He's

wrangled the boys so I could come back and say congrats. Are you staying in town long?"

"Another week, maybe a bit longer. I have some things I need to do at the gallery, and honestly, we can use the break."

"So, I'll get to see lots of you?"

"Yes, I promise."

Beth walked away but glanced back over her shoulder. Chase had wrapped his arms around Sophie and was kissing her, oblivious to everyone else in the room. She turned back around and smiled. Chase was just what Sophie needed.

HARRISON DROPPED Nora off at her cabin late that night and walked her to the door. She was almost getting used to climbing out of his ever-so-low sports car. Almost.

"Would you like to come inside? Maybe have a glass of wine?"

"I'd like that."

She was probably crazy, because it was already later than she usually stayed up and she had to be up early tomorrow, but she just didn't want the day to end. And that...

bothered her. Because she'd already decided there was nothing between Harrison and her. Nothing.

And yet… she wanted him to stay.

She poured glasses of wine, and they went to sit out on the porch swing. The chair gently swayed and they sat in silence, staring out into the quiet darkness.

"I had a really good time today." She wasn't sure why she was admitting it to him.

"I did, too." He shifted in the swing to look at her. "A really, *really* good time." He reached and took her wineglass and placed their glasses on the worn planks of the porch.

Her heart began to pound.

He reached out and touched her cheek, ever so gently, then brushed her hair away from her face. "I want to kiss you again."

"You do?" Her pulse was racing so fast she could barely catch her breath.

"Very much so." He touched her cheek.

"I—"

"I'm just waiting for you to ask me to kiss you." His finger trailed along her lips.

Her mind and heart quarreled. Her rational, practical side argued with her let's-just-jump-in side.

His finger stilled, and he looked directly at her, waiting.

"Kiss me." She closed her eyes and soon felt his lips on hers. Then she forgot about what she was worried about, forgot what her practical side had said.

She forgot everything except for his kiss.

CHAPTER 24

Harrison sat in his cabin the next morning after doing some more research on Blue Horizon Company. He scrolled through the photos on his phone that he'd taken of the papers in Walt's office at the cabin. He paused when he got to the list of investors.

Gloria Edmonds.

That's why her name sounded familiar to him.

He jumped up from the table. Yesterday, he'd meant to tell Nora what he'd found out about the sale, but they'd gotten to talking and he hadn't wanted to disturb the fragile camaraderie they'd shared with talk of the sale and rezoning.

But now he needed to tell her everything.

No secrets. And he was sure she'd be interested to know that Gloria was behind some of her problems.

He hurried over to the lodge and saw Jason working the front desk. "Hey, I'm looking for your mother."

"I think she headed up to the gazebo on the ridge. She goes up there sometimes when she needs time to think." Jason eyed him. "She seemed... um... pensive this morning. Everything okay between you two?"

Harrison didn't know what to say to him. It wasn't his place to talk to Nora's son about their shared kissed. So he just shrugged.

"Anyway, go out that door and there's a path up to the top of the ridge. Can't miss it."

He hurried outside and climbed the trail to the top of the ridge. Nora stood at the railing of the gazebo, looking out over the lake and the mountains in the distance. She turned when she heard him approach, and he was rewarded with a smile.

He crossed the wooden planks and stood beside her. "Hey." He covered her hand resting on the railing.

"Hi." She smiled at him again.

He thought he could just stand here all day

and look at that smile of hers. The smile that reached all the way to her amber eyes.

She nodded toward the lake. "Quite a view here, isn't it?"

"It is. I'm thinking you know all the great views around these parts."

"I'm a view collector," she said seriously, paused, then grinned.

His phone dinged, and he took it out of his pocket and looked at it. Yet another text from Walt asking if his mother had signed the papers. He turned off the phone, determined to not let Walt interrupt this time with Nora.

"So, I need to talk to you. Do you have time now?"

She looked up at him with curiosity in her eyes. "I do."

He led her over to a bench and they sat next to each other. "So... I did some investigating. Well, actually I went to my grandfather's cabin and poked around. I mean I had every right to be there..."

"You do." She nodded.

"But I still felt a bit guilty. But anyway, I found some paperwork and now I know for certain he's cheating my mother."

"What did she say when you told her?"

"Haven't been able to reach her. She rarely carries her cell phone. If I don't reach her tonight, I'll have someone at the retirement center have her call me." He took Nora's hand in his, pleased she didn't pull away when he did. "There's more. It appears that Walt is actually one of the investors in the company buying the property. He's selling for a low price because he'll make his money on the sale of the condos. And he's guaranteed a penthouse condo for life, rent-free."

Nora shook her head. "Walt's always got an angle."

"And there's more…" He squeezed her hand. "Gloria Edmonds is one of the investors, too."

Nora sat silent for a moment, then stood and walked over to the railing. He got up to go stand beside her.

"That woman is always trying to make things harder for me. I shouldn't be surprised that she's involved in all this."

He so wanted to reach out and smooth the creases of the frown firmly etched on her face.

Nora let out a long sigh. "But I'm not sure how this knowledge is going to change anything, except possibly get your mother her fair share, which she deserves."

"I'm fairly certain my mother won't sign the sale. She's not going to want the cabin torn down. Or condos. She loves this lake... almost as much as you do."

He was rewarded with another smile.

"I have to admit, nothing would make me happier than the sale not going through."

"I've got a good idea." He took her hand.

"What's that?"

"Let's get away for a while. How about you take me on a hike to one of those famous views of yours. I wouldn't mind just forgetting all about this for a bit."

"Now that sounds like a fabulous idea. Let's go to our cabins and change into hiking gear, and I'll meet you at my cabin in half an hour. Oh, and I'm driving." Nora turned and headed back down the ridge and he followed in her wake, glad he'd suggested the outing and pleased to be spending more time with her.

NORA WAS STRANGELY PLEASED with Harrison's suggestion to get away for a bit. She was going to take him to Lost Lake, another one of her favorite views of the area. And she was driving because she was good and tired of climbing in and out of his ridiculous sports car. Who drove a sports car in the mountains, anyway?

Precisely thirty minutes later, Harrison showed up at her door in jeans, flannel shirt, and hiking shoes. He looked… good. Very good. She liked him so much better in this casual attire than his stuffy business outfits he usually wore. Well, he used to wear. She'd noticed he'd gotten more casual as he stayed here longer.

She drove them to the trailhead for the path up Grace's Peak. "We start here, and then a trail veers off between Grace's Peak and Sky View Mountain and heads to Lost Lake."

He laughed. "Well, I'll just follow you."

They hiked along the pathway until they got to the ridge that cut between Grace's Peak and Sky View Mountain. She paused there and let Harrison take in the view. Down in the valley between the mountains, the sunlight glistened off the surface of the lake. At the far end, a waterfall fed the lake.

He let out a low whistle. "This is gorgeous. Can't believe I never came here as a kid. Though I wasn't much of a hiker back then."

"You weren't?" She eyed him.

"I was the pudgy nerd. Out of shape."

She looked at his trim, fit body and couldn't reconcile it with an overweight nerdy boy.

He laughed. "Yes, I was the fat kid everyone made fun of."

"Just can't see it." She shook her head.

"Truth." He shrugged. "In college I started working out. Started eating healthy. And I think part of the weight was just how I was as a boy. Outgrew it. And, well, I worked hard on getting into shape. Which I'll have to do again when I leave here after eating all these delicious but fattening meals."

"Well, hiking will help with that." She turned and led them down the trail that dropped them beside Lost Lake. They sat on some boulders beside the lake to rest. She took a water bottle out of her backpack and handed it to Harrison. His long fingers wrapped around the container, and he took a long swallow. The sun lit up the few strands of gray in his hair, only making him look more handsome as far as she was concerned.

Not that it concerned her *one bit* if he was handsome or not.

CHAPTER 25

Harrison couldn't remember when he'd had such a good, relaxing time, even with all the exercise. And exercising by taking a hike was a much more excellent way to get back into shape than running on a treadmill, watching the news on the monitor at the gym.

They slowly made their way back to Nora's car and headed back to the lodge. He was sorry to see the outing end, but he knew she had to get back to work. He needed to call the retirement home and see if he could finally talk to his mother. Then he'd deal with Walt.

He walked Nora inside when they got to the lodge. Jason was still working at the front desk. "Oh, hey, Harrison. Did your mom catch up with you?"

"My mother? Did she call here looking for me?"

"Call? No, she was here looking for you."

He took in a quick breath. Why hadn't she told him she was coming? He pulled out his phone. No messages from her.

"Did she look okay?"

Jason looked at him strangely. "She looked fine to me."

This was something he hadn't expected but should have. His mother did like to take care of things herself when she could. Well, the good news was she must be feeling better. "Do you know where she is now?"

"She said something about visiting her nephew. That would be Walt, right?"

He whirled around to Nora. "I've got to go. I don't trust Walt a bit."

"Here, I'll drive you." They hurried off to her car, and she quickly drove to the cabin. When they pulled up to the cabin, Harrison jumped out of the car and hurried up to the front door. He tugged it open without even knocking.

His mother was sitting at the desk in Grandfather's office, a pen in hand. Walt hovered at her side. She looked up when he strode into the room. "Oh, Harrison, dear. There you are."

"Mother, what are you doing here? Are you sure you're up to travel?"

"Of course I am. You don't think a little bout of pneumonia would sideline me for long, did you? I told the doctor I was perfectly fine to travel. End of discussion."

She did look perfectly healthy and not even exhausted from her travels.

"What are you doing?"

"Signing the sale papers. Walt told me you agreed it's a fair deal."

He strode up to the desk and grabbed the papers. There was his mother's signature, clear as day. He threw the papers back on the desk. "Only, it's not a fair deal and Walt knows it. And they're going to tear down the cabin and put up condos."

His mother stood, her eyes flashing. She turned and faced Walt. "Walter, is that true?"

"Well, I'm not sure what the buyer's plans are…" he faltered.

"Except that *you* are one of the buyers," Harrison interjected, his pulse racing. How dare Walter trick his mother into signing?

"But why would Walt buy this property

when he owns it now?" His mother looked confused.

Walter's eyes widened. "I—why do you think that?"

"Because you are. You're an investor in Blue Horizon. Along with Chuck Smith and Gloria Edmonds and a few others I don't recognize, but I bet Nora would."

Nora came to stand beside him and rested a hand on his arm, a show of support.

"Well, it doesn't matter. Aunt Ellen signed the papers. It's a done deal." Walt snatched the paper from the desk and held it close.

"Pretty sure a judge might rule against that…" Harrison narrowed his eyes.

"Well, you can try. But I bet it stands. And even if it doesn't, in the event of a disagreement, my signature will be enough."

"What are you talking about?" Harrison took a step toward Walt, fury raging through him.

"If there are no other descendants—and neither of us has children—I get to break any tie or disagreement on disposal of the property."

"Disposal?" His mother's eyes flashed. "*Disposal?* This property that has been in the family for generations. You want to *dispose* of it?"

"And where did you get that cockamamie idea that you get to decide? That's not in the will." Harrison balled his hands into fist, struggling to keep control.

"But it is in a letter I found in Grandfather's safe. His wishes if there is a disagreement. I was here when he wrote it before he died."

"I bet you were." Yet another one of Walt's tricks. "I'll file an injunction tomorrow to stop the sale."

Walter smirked. "Try it. The letter will hold up in court. Signed by Grandfather, Vernon Dobbs. It's even notarized. I was just trying to let Aunt Ellen sign to make things easier on the family. And she did sign, actually. But if that signature gets overturned, I'll still get the right to sell the property."

His mother turned to him. "I'm sorry. I shouldn't have believed Walter. He lied to me. He's lied before… I feel like such an old fool."

"Mom, none of this is your fault."

"What does it matter now, anyway?" Walt actually laughed.

"The truth always matters," Nora insisted.

"Come on, Mother. We're leaving." He took

his mother's arm and led her out of the cabin with Nora following close behind them.

His mother took a long look at the cabin as they walked out. "I don't want to lose this, Harrison. So much history. So many memories."

"I'll do everything that I can to make sure you don't." But he had no clue how he was going to do that.

HE AND HIS mother followed Nora in his mom's rental car. When they got to the lodge, Nora came up and held out her hand to his mother. "We didn't have time to get introduced in all that mess. I'm Nora Cassidy."

"Nice to meet you, Nora. I guess by now you've figured out I'm Ellen Stanworth, Harrison's mother."

"I bet you could use a rest after the day you've had."

"I could. I'm just so shocked at all Walter would do to trick a family member and cheat them."

Harrison hated seeing the hurt in his mother's eyes. But he wasn't surprised at what

Walt had done. Not one bit. Because he'd done it before, and Harrison had been gullible enough to believe him…

"How about I move you two to a bigger cabin? There's a nice one with two master bedrooms near the lodge."

Harrison wasn't sure he wanted to give up his little cabin on the lake near the magical grove of Aspens, but it would be better for his mother.

"I don't need anything special," his mom protested.

"No, the cabin will be perfect for you two. We'll just get Harrison's things moved over to it."

Nora left to go get the new keys for them. His mother sat on one of the pine benches while they waited. He worried about her. She was starting to look tired.

Just then Linda walked past them. His mother stared at her as she walked past, then leaned close to him. "Do you know that woman?"

"Barely. Her name is Linda. Linda Seabridge."

His mother frowned. "Name doesn't sound familiar, but there's something about her…"

A strange feeling skittered through him. His mother had the exact same feeling about Linda as he did. But he just couldn't believe he'd met her before. And wouldn't she have said something if they had? Though she *had* been sneaking around the cabin. Maybe she was somehow tied into the deal that Walt had made.

Nora came up to them and interrupted his thoughts. "Here are the new keys. Why don't you get your mother settled? I can send someone over to move your things if you want."

"No, I'll help Mother and let her take a little rest, then I'll go get my things."

Nora's fingers brushed his as she handed him the keys. He shot her a grateful look. "Thanks."

She smiled encouragingly at him and nodded as if giving him her silent support.

"Come on, Mom. Let's get you all settled. You'll love it here."

His mother stood and took his arm. "I'm sure I will. The lodge looks charming. Thank you, Nora."

"You're welcome."

He led his mother away toward the door. He glanced back over his shoulder, and Nora was still standing there, watching them. He opened the door, and he and his mother walked outside.

A sudden longing for Nora hit him as soon as the door closed behind him.

NORA DROPPED by Harrison and Ellen's cabin after finishing up in the dining hall that evening. She knocked softly, not wanting to disturb Ellen if she was already asleep. She'd had quite an afternoon on top of a day of travel.

Harrison opened the door, and soft light spilled out onto the porch. "Nora." His eyes held a grateful look.

"I just wanted to check on you and make sure you didn't need anything."

"No, we're good. Mom's already in bed." He paused and looked at her. "Would you like to come in for a bit?"

"We could sit out here on the porch so we don't bother your mother."

He nodded, stepped outside, and closed the door behind him. She sat on an Adirondack chair while he lounged against the railing.

"So is your mother doing okay?"

"She's devastated that she let Walt trick her.

But I'm fairly certain I can get her signature overturned. But if that document he has holds up… I'm not sure it will do any good."

She got back up and went to stand by him at the railing. "I'm so sorry for all of this."

"None of it is your fault."

"I still feel bad for both of you."

"Know what would make me feel better?" He cocked his head.

"No. What?"

"A kiss." He flashed her a boyish grin.

"Oh, then. We want you to feel better." She stood on tiptoes and pressed a quick kiss on his lips.

His arms wrapped around her and he held her close. She rested her cheek against his chest, feeling his heartbeat. They stood like that for a long time, neither one of them wanting to break the connection.

CHAPTER 26

Nora climbed to the loft at Bookish Cafe the next day, looking for Annie. She found her sitting beside a window.

"Since when do you knit?"

"Since Nancy has been holding knitting classes here at Bookish Cafe. I find it rather soothing."

"What are you making?" Nora eyed the mint green square.

"A baby blanket?"

"For who?"

"Well, I figure with both Beth and Jason just getting married, it won't be long until you have some more grandchildren." Annie grinned. "And at the speed I knit, it's going to take me a while to get a couple of baby blankets finished."

Nora laughed and took a seat beside her. "That's my Annie. Always prepared."

"So, what brings you to town?" Annie's knitting needles stilled, and she grinned sheepishly. "I can't talk and knit yet. Have to concentrate."

"Ah, so much to tell you." She proceeded to tell Annie about the mess with Walt and Harrison's mom and the sale. "So Harrison is filing an injunction to stop Walt, but I'm not sure if it will do any good. His mother is so distraught."

"Walt and the judge are good buddies. That's not going to help much."

"Not without a lot of appeals." She sighed.

"Walt can never be trusted, can he?" Annie paused and looked at her closely. "And now you're going to tell me that Harrison kissed you, aren't you?"

Nora laughed in surprise. "I wasn't... but he did."

"Knew it." A self-satisfied look crossed Annie's face, then she frowned. "You're still not all mixed up about your feelings for him, are you?"

She sighed. "Pretty much. I mean, I enjoy spending time with him. I like him..."

"You care about him. You're falling for him," Annie added.

She grinned. "That, too. But it's… complicated."

"Life always is."

"Oh, that reminds me. Complications. There's more to the Walter story."

"What?" Annie's eyes showed she knew Nora was deliberately changing the subject.

"Gloria Edmonds is one of the buyers, too."

Annie set her knitting on the side table and jumped to her feet. "Gloria? I'm so tired of Gloria Edmonds. She's always at the bottom of our troubles."

Nora stood and hugged her friend. "But at least the first time she made trouble for you, something good came out of it."

"What's that?"

"You became my very best lifelong friend."

Annie smiled and hugged her back. No matter how things got muddled in life, they'd always be there for each other.

HARRISON WALKED out of the lawyer's office after meeting with him the next morning. Things didn't look very promising. The lawyer was fairly certain a judge would overturn his mother's signature and they could prove she was lied to and coerced. But if the letter Walt had held up in court, it might not matter if his mother signed or not. The lawyer made no promises but said he'd do some research.

It was all so frustrating. How could it be legal for Walt to cheat his mother like this? And why would his grandfather have signed that letter giving Walt the right to decide if there was a disagreement? He sighed. Walt had probably tricked his grandfather, too. The man was not above doing *anything* when it came to preserving his own interests.

He headed back to the lodge and ran into Nora and his mother.

Nora smiled at him as soon as she saw him. A flutter of hope flickered through him. Just seeing her made him feel better.

"We were just going to sit out on the porch and have some iced tea." Nora held up a tray with a pitcher of tea and two glasses. "Want to join us?"

"I do. Let me go grab another glass." He

hurried into the dining hall and grabbed a clean glass from the sideboard.

"Hey, Harrison." Jason walked out of the kitchen.

"Hi." He held up his glass. "Going to join Mom and Nora for some iced tea."

"Sounds good. Another sunny, warm fall day. We're really lucky this year. Some years we've already had snow by now. Supposed to get that first snowfall any day now, though."

"Well, I'll take these kinds of days."

"So—" Jason paused.

"Yes?"

"Well… I just wanted to say. I mean." Jason sighed. "Look, I don't want my mother getting hurt."

"I don't want her getting hurt either."

"But… you're leaving and she's staying, and… like I said, I don't want her hurt."

He stared at the man for a moment. The concern was clear in Jason's eyes. "I don't know where things are going with your mother, but I do care about her."

Jason nodded. "Just—be careful with her. Please. She's already dealt with a lot in life. She doesn't need any more pain."

"I hear you." He nodded and turned to leave.

"Just think about it." Jason's words followed him out of the dining hall.

CHAPTER 27

Linda knew she shouldn't be eavesdropping, but she couldn't help herself. She sat on a chair just around the corner from where Harrison, Nora, and another woman were sitting and talking, and she couldn't help but overhear what they were talking about.

"The lawyer said we're going to have quite a battle with Walt, and it could get pretty expensive."

"I don't care what it costs. I will not have my nephew lying and tricking me like that. I feel like a foolish old lady," the woman said.

Linda sat up straight. Her nephew was Walt? She must be Harrison's mother, then. She was... Linda reached up, her hand over her heart, and closed her eyes. Emotions soared through her, and she swallowed, trying to gain control.

"Well, if Walt's letter says if the descendants disagree on the disposition of the property, then he gets to decide... well, we'll lose. We'll lose everything. The cabin, the property, and you'll only get that laughable amount for your share, Mom."

"I feel like this is all my fault." The woman —she must be Ellen—answered.

Linda opened her eyes and took in a deep breath.

It was time.

She stood and slowly walked around the corner of the porch and up to the trio. "We should talk."

Harrison looked at her in surprise, his eyes narrowed. "What do you want?"

"I—I would like you to listen to me for a few minutes. Please."

"Of course, dear. Sit." Ellen motioned to a chair beside her.

Harrison didn't look nearly as agreeable.

Nora stayed silent and sipped her tea, watching.

She took a seat, rubbed her hands on her jeans and swallowed again. "I—well—"

"Go ahead dear, take your time." Ellen smiled encouragingly.

Harrison scowled.

"Vernon—your grandfather—" She looked at Harrison. "And your father—" She nodded at Ellen. "He grew up next door to my mother. He and Mom's brother—my Uncle John—were best friends. Mom was ten years younger than them, tagging along, bothering them, and I think she always had a secret school-girl crush on your grandfather."

Harrison sat forward in his chair, a crease of concentration between his eyebrows.

"About a year or so after your grandmother died, Mom and Uncle John were traveling through Colorado and stopped to see Vernon. Check on him and see how he was doing. Uncle John went back home, and I guess my mother ended up staying in Sweet River Falls for a while. And, well, I guess they—my mom and Vernon—got… close."

Harrison sat his glass of tea down with a resounding thud. Ellen frowned.

"Mom didn't fully explain, but I think

Vernon began to feel guilty like he was cheating on his wife—even though she was gone—or maybe he just wasn't ready for a real relationship. He broke up with my mom. My mom was a very proud woman. When she found out she was pregnant, she didn't tell Vernon. She decided to raise me alone. But then she met my dad... well, *now* I know he wasn't really my father. They moved to a new city and told everyone I was his daughter. I was too young to know the difference. They never told me the truth. They both kept Mom's secret for all those years."

Harrison looked like he didn't believe her, and she couldn't blame him. She could barely believe the story herself. Everything she believed about her life and her family had been a lie.

She took another deep breath. "But when my Mom was on hospice, she gave me these papers. It was such a shock. The man I thought was my father—Barry—he wasn't. He died a few years ago, then Mom died..." She swallowed. "It was just two months ago." Tears rolled down her face, and she slashed at them with the side of her hand. She'd lost so many people in the last few years. So many deaths. So alone.

Well, *almost* alone.

She struggled to get back in control of her emotions. Ellen reached over and patted her hand. "Take your time."

Harrison sat in shock but still held a disbelieving look in his eyes.

"Somewhere in there, Vernon came looking for my mom. But by then she was married to my father— to Barry. She told Vernon the truth about me. I do remember him coming to visit a few times, but not that he was my father. He was just this old friend of my mom's that visited every now and again. I remember his laugh was deep and rumbled through the room. He had the kindest eyes, I remember that. They were the color of the ocean. But his eyes had the saddest look about them."

"That's why you look familiar. I've met your mother once at the cabin. Her name was Patricia, wasn't it?" Ellen leaned forward in her chair.

Linda nodded. "Yes." And even though she was mad at her mother for keeping this secret all these years, it felt good to be talking to someone who actually knew her mother. Her emotions rolled over her such that she had a hard time taking a breath.

"You look just like her... except... you have

my father's eyes. And ocean blue is the exact way to describe them." Ellen reached out and took Linda's hands in hers. "So you're my younger sister?"

Linda held on tightly, glad to have the opportunity to share this story with someone. "Well, half-sister, and quite a bit younger, I'm afraid. I'm younger than your own son."

"Well, my parents were only eighteen when they had me. And mother died so young, when Harrison was just a young boy. I'm not surprised my father had a relationship with someone new. He would have only been about mid-forties then." Ellen squeezed her hand. "He had such a tough time after mother died. I'm glad he had Patricia to turn to, but I'm sorry it's taken us all this time to find you."

Harrison stood and glared at her. "And we're supposed to take your word about all of this?" He walked to the railing, then paced back toward his chair.

"No, I don't suppose you are. But I have proof."

He turned around to stare at her. "Proof?"

"Vernon added me to his will and gave a copy of it to my mother. It... he... well, he names me specifically. Mom gave me the documents before she died. I have the papers with me. I can show you."

"I believe you, dear." Ellen squeezed her hand.

"I'm going to need to see those papers." Harrison sat down in his chair and stared at her.

"I'll be right back." She got up and headed back to her cabin, trying to calm her rolling nerves and trying to get enough oxygen back into her lungs so she could think straight. She'd finally told someone else the truth. She had a half-sister. She pressed her hand against her belly. And her baby would have a family too… *if* they'd accept her and her child.

"I don't believe her. What a coincidence she turns up now." Harrison jumped up from his seat he'd just taken.

Nora watched as he paced up and down the worn boards of the porch. "She says she has proof. Why not wait to see what she brings you?"

"I believe her." Ellen sat still. "I think my father started to tell me the truth about all this one time. He mentioned he'd revised his will, but we got interrupted by Walt, and whatever he was going to tell me, it was obvious he didn't want to share with him. He died soon after that."

"I'm having a hard time imagining Grandfather with someone other than Grandmother."

"He was desperately lonely after Mom died. So lonely. I certainly don't judge him for wanting a friend or companion. And I could see how he might feel guilty like he was betraying Mom's memory."

Nora could so empathize with the man. She glanced at Harrison knowing full well that her own guilt was what was standing between her and Harrison and any chance they had at... well, anything. Or even trying to figure what they had between them. Old Vernon Dobbs wasn't the only one who got tangled up in memories and new feelings.

"But why wouldn't Grandfather tell us? Why keep a secret?"

"Maybe since Patricia had married and her husband had taken Linda as his own. Maybe out of respect for that decision? Plus, he probably regretted he sent her away."

Linda came back around the corner of the

porch. She walked up to Harrison and thrust the papers at him. "Here."

He took the papers and walked to the edge of the porch and slowly pored over them. Ellen patted the chair beside her, and Linda sat.

Nora watched while Harrison scanned the pages. One after the next. She knew the exact moment that he believed Linda. She could see it in the set of his shoulders. He turned to Linda.

"It appears that everything you said is true. There's this letter from Grandfather—and I recognize his writing—along with his revised will. Everything notarized." He walked over to her and dropped down beside her. "I'm sorry I didn't believe you. I know *all* of this... *nothing* of this..." He let out a long breath. "I guess I just want to say, welcome to the family."

Tears ran down Linda's face, and she didn't try to hide them. Ellen took Linda's hand in hers. "Yes, dear. You're family now."

Harrison looked at Linda and gave her a wry smile. "Unfortunately, Walt also comes with this family."

CHAPTER 28

Harrison looked at the petite woman sitting before him, trying to wipe away her tears. He rocked back on his heels. "I can't imagine what a shock this must have been for you to find out all of this while... while your mother was dying."

"It was. I had so many emotions. Sadness, surprise, anger. I guess I still do." She rested her hands in her lap as her tears subsided. "I'm sure it's been just as big a shock to you."

He stood and went to lean on the railing. "I'm shocked, I admit. It's kind of strange to have an aunt who's younger than I am, but... well, nothing about the last few days has been normal."

"Well, I'm happy to have a sister after all

these years." His mother smiled, always gracious.

He frowned. "This changes things quite a bit."

"What do you mean, dear?"

"Well, Walt doesn't have the final say on what happens to the property and the cabin. A sale would need all three of you to sign. And once we show the new will and Grandfather's letter, there would need to be a new sale document."

Ellen jumped up. "You mean we might not lose the cabin?" She turned to Linda. "Oh, but maybe you'd want to sell?"

Linda shook her head. "I had actually hoped to be able to spend some time there. Maybe get a feel for what Vernon was like. I was shocked to hear the rumor in town that Walter was planning on selling the land."

"Not only the land... but they're going to tear down that lovely cabin." His mother's eyes clouded. "But now... maybe we could stop him."

Harrison explained to Linda the whole story about Walt tricking his mother into signing and how he had a paper that said if the remaining descendants didn't have a majority agreement, that Walt could decide on the sale.

"But now we have three people who have inheritance rights to the land." Linda looked out across the porch at the view of the lake. "And Walter wants to put up condos on the land and tear down the cabin?"

"That's his plan. And he's cheated my mother out of a fair sale price, too."

"I'm not so sure I like this new nephew of mine."

"You're in good company." Harrison scowled.

"Well, I know I'm new to the family, but I have no desire to sell the property or the cabin. I'd love to be able to come here to visit. Get to know the area where Vernon—my father— lived." She turned to look at Ellen. "If that's okay with you."

"That sounds wonderful to me. I'd like to come spend time at the cabin, too, and get to know you better." His mother smiled, her eyes shining. "Who knew I could get an actual sister at this stage of my life?"

"I think we should all go pay Walt a visit tomorrow." Harrison laughed. "I'm thinking he's going to be pretty surprised by this new turn of events."

NORA SAT outside Harrison's cabin again that evening after they'd all had a big dinner at the lodge. Linda had returned to her own cabin, and Ellen had retired to her bedroom. She sat beside Harrison as they sipped on some red wine.

"It was quite a day, wasn't it?" Nora could see how tired Harrison's eyes looked.

"It was."

"But now you'll get to keep the land and the cabin. Ellen looked so pleased."

"She did look happy, didn't she? I think the idea of losing the cabin was really distressing her."

"And she looked so happy to meet Linda and have the chance to get to know her. Did you hear the two of them talking at dinner? All about knitting and then about some book series they'd both read? I think they said it was called Lighthouse Point? Anyway, I think they're going to get along fabulously." Nora took a sip of wine. "But I don't think Walt is going to take the news very well."

"And I don't care one bit about how Walt takes the news."

"There's no love lost between you two, is there?"

"No…" Harrison looked out into the night. "At one time we were friends. Well, I thought we were. I tried to be. He'd sometimes let me tag along with him and his friends when I came here in the summer."

He turned and looked at her, his eyes sad and haunted. "Then my last summer here… there was a terrible accident. Walt took my grandfather's car. He and his buddies took it out joyriding. He ran into a tree and totaled the car. One of the boys was hurt badly. He was in the hospital for months recovering."

She frowned. "But your grandfather gave Walt the power to make the decision if the inheritors couldn't agree?"

Harrison stood and walked over to the railing. "I'm not sure that Walt didn't trick Grandfather into signing that letter, and Grandfather never found out that it was Walt driving the car."

"He didn't?"

"Walt told him it was me."

"But you told him it wasn't, didn't you? Didn't he believe you?"

"I never did say it wasn't me. I didn't say anything. I just let him think it was me."

"Why in the world would you do that?" She chewed her lip, not understanding.

"Because Walt had me convinced that my mother was cheating on my Dad. Said he'd tell my father. He even had a photo of her with another man that he showed me. Said he'd followed her and spied on her and took the photos. I was just—in shock." He paced the porch. "I didn't want my dad's world to blow up, and I didn't want my family to break up. So I stayed silent. Walt said it was best for me to take the blame because he lived in Sweet River Falls and he had a scholarship to play football at college in the fall and it might ruin things if it got out that he'd done this. And his buddies all backed up his story. Anyway, I stayed silent to protect my family."

"And your grandfather never found out?"

"I'm not sure."

"After it happened, my grandfather yelled at me about how irresponsible I was and how someone could have been killed and how disappointed he was in me. He paid the hospital bill for Walt's friend. And…" Harrison paused in his pacing, his eyes full of pain. "And my grandfather sent me away. Told me not to come back."

"Oh, Harrison." Her heart broke for the boy he'd been, banished from a place he loved, and the man standing before her, still haunted by the memory.

"When Mom heard what happened she went to talk to Grandfather. I know my mother defended me. She just didn't believe I would do that. Take the car like that and be so irresponsible. But I never told her the truth because… well, I still thought I was protecting her." His eyes narrowed. "Then years later I found that exact same picture of my mother and that man. Turns out he was a second cousin or second cousin once or twice removed or something like that. They'd met at a family reunion years ago and he still stopped by to see her when he came to town. And now I'm sure Walt knew that but lied to me to get what he wanted. I feel terrible that I believed his lies about my mother."

"And you never came back to Sweet River Falls?"

"No, I couldn't. Grandfather told me to leave and stay away. I didn't return until this trip"

"Well, it looks like Walt is getting what's coming to him tomorrow. And I have to say, I'm not sorry. He's a mean-hearted man. And I'm the first to admit I'm beyond thrilled that there won't be condos built right across from us on the lake."

He smiled at her then and took her hand. "I'm glad for you too. The lake is beautiful, isn't it? Magical." He leaned over and kissed her, and the feelings that swept through her took her breath away.

It was a magical place. A very magical place.

CHAPTER 29

First thing the next morning, Harrison took his mother, Linda, and Nora over to Walt's place. It *wasn't Walt's* place. He had to keep reminding himself. It was his grandfather's cabin. Well, it was owned three ways by Walt, Linda, and his mother. He grinned as he pulled up to the cabin.

He knocked on the door and watched Walt's eyes widen as he opened the door. Walt frowned. "What do you want?"

"We're coming in," his mother said forcefully.

He had to hide a smile at her spunk. Now *that's* the mother he remembered and adored.

"I'm busy."

"That's okay. We have every right to be

here." His mother brushed passed Walter, pulling Linda along with her.

Harrison took Nora's arm, and they walked into the cabin.

"What's this all about? I talked to my lawyer in Denver. He said my claim is legal even if you get Aunt Ellen's signature on the sale overturned. *I* get to decide what we're doing with the property."

Harrison turned when Gloria Edmonds walked out of his grandfather's office.

"Walter, what's all this?" She stood with a hand on her hip, not looking pleased.

"They're just poor losers." Walt smirked.

"Actually, we came to show you this." Harrison held out a copy of the amended will.

Walt glanced at it and didn't look all that surprised by what he read. "This is obviously a fake."

"No, it's not. And it's notarized *and* we have this letter from Grandfather, too."

Harrison looked past Walt into the open door to the office. His grandfather's safe was wide open. He quickly walked past Walt, into the office, and directly over to the safe. Walt looked up and lumbered into the office. "Hey, get out of there."

Harrison scooped out the papers in the safe. "It's not technically your safe, Walt."

"Yes, it is…" Walt sputtered.

Harrison looked at the papers in his hand. A copy of the very same amended will that he'd just given to Walt. He looked at his cousin. "How did you get this?" He shook his head. "Never mind. Just another lie and trick. So you knew all along that there was another person who had rights to the property."

"No, I—"

"Oh, stop." His mother walked up beside him. "Is that a copy of the will Linda had?"

"It is."

"Walter, you've done nothing but try to destroy this family. Your father would have been devastated to know the man you've become."

Gloria walked into the office. "What does this mean, Walter? Is the sale not going to go through? I already sold my house. I was so tired of the upkeep. I was depending on having a condo here on the lake with people to take care of all that for me. All I have now is a temporary rental."

"Looks like you should look for more permanent housing." Harrison rolled his eyes.

He glanced at Nora and didn't miss the quickly hidden smile that crossed her face.

"And Walter, we're going to use the cabin as a family retreat from now on. I think it best if you found yourself a new place to live," his mother insisted.

"But this is my home," Walt practically whined.

"No, it's not. And unless you'd like to pay the family foundation back rent for all the years you've lived here… then I suggest you find new lodging. We can decide how the cabin is used since two out of the three descendants agree. You know, as per the new will." His mother walked up to Walt. "You have two weeks."

"Two weeks?"

"That's more than generous considering all the lies you've told and the secrets you've kept. Enough is enough. I refuse to let one family member ruin what a wonderful family we had… and still do have." She turned and smiled at Linda.

"Walter, do something." Gloria stood with her arms on her hips, eyes flashing.

"There's really nothing your good friend Walt can do at this point." Harrison shook his head.

"You're all fools, you know. The will says if there are no descendants left, the property will go to the town. In case you've forgotten, neither you nor I have any kids. And I already checked. Linda here doesn't either. You're giving up all that money we could split if we sell now. The town will eventually get the property and we'll get nothing. They may even decide to put up condos here. So you've just delayed the inevitable."

It didn't surprise him that Walt already knew about Linda specifically and had checked her out. *Nothing* Walt did surprised him anymore.

Linda walked up to him and held up a hand. "Let me say something." She turned to Walt. "And yet, I will have a child in five more months." She rested her hand on her belly.

Walter's eyes went wide. "But your husband died."

Harrison looked at Linda in surprise. She'd lost her mother *and* her husband?

"He did. And right afterward I found out I was pregnant." Tears clouded her eyes, but she stood tall. "It was a surprise, but a wonderful surprise."

Harrison was pretty darn proud of this new

aunt of his. His mother came over and hugged Linda. "Oh, Linda. This is such exciting news."

"I wanted to come here and find out about my family. My baby's family. That's why I came to Sweet River Falls. It's a bit late in life to have a child, but the doctor said that both the baby and I are doing fine. And I count this child as a real blessing. A gift from my husband."

"As well you should. A child is always a blessing," his mother agreed.

"Walter?" Gloria still stood glaring at all of them.

"I think it best if you leave now, Walter. You can come back later for your personal items, but I'll be here to make sure that's all you take." His mother stood next to Linda, her arm protectively around her shoulder. "Linda is going to get to know this wonderful place. And all its history. And your lies and trickery will no longer be tolerated, do you hear me?"

Walt almost looked chastened. Almost. "Come on, Gloria. Let's go." Walter took Gloria's arm and led her toward the door.

"Seriously, Walter. Where am I going to live?" Gloria's annoyed voice filtered through the room.

"Where am *I* going to live?" Walter muttered under his breath.

And maybe it made him a shallow, ungracious man, but Harrison just didn't care where Walt ended up.

HARRISON SAT at the desk in his grandfather's office. Nora had taken his mother and Linda back to the lodge, but he'd wanted to stay and sort through the papers here. He didn't really want any more surprises.

He riffled through the papers he'd taken from the safe and saw an envelope addressed to him. In his grandfather's handwriting. Yet something else Walt had hidden from him.

He swallowed and slowly opened the envelope, the glue no longer sealing it, or maybe it had been opened before.

With shaking hands, he unfolded the paper and smoothed it on the desk.

My Dearest Harrison,

. . .

I HAVE many regrets in my life, not the least of which is sending you away all those years ago. I should have known that you had nothing to do with the accident. When I got so sick, that Meyer boy who was hurt in the accident finally came and told me the truth. Told me Walter had been driving the car. I guess he felt guilty I'd die not knowing the truth and wanted to ease his own conscience.

But now my health is failing, and if you're reading this, I am gone. I've left instructions to make sure you get this letter along with the new will.

I want you to know that I have another daughter, Linda. She's a lovely young woman. It's a long story that is hers or her mother's to tell. I hope that you will make sure she and her mother get their rightful inheritance from my estate. I've enclosed information on how you can find them.

And I want to offer my deepest regrets, I am so very sorry for how I handled the situation. You're a fine man and I love you. Please accept my very belated apology. I know my apology won't change how things turned out, but I still want you to know how sorry I am.

Never let things go unsaid to someone you love.

My love and affection always,

GRANDFATHER

. . .

HARRISON BLINKED BACK the tears that threatened to spill. The words he'd waited half his lifetime to hear. That his grandfather loved him. He clutched the paper to his chest and walked out onto the porch, looking out over the lake. He sucked in a deep breath of the clean air and looked at the mountains in the distance with the first snowfall of the year just covering their peaks. He could feel the approaching snowfall in the air.

And he could almost feel his grandfather standing beside him.

"I forgive you, Grandfather." He whispered the words across the lake.

CHAPTER 30

Nora and Harrison sat on a bench beside the lake that evening. A full moon flooded the area with its silvery light. Harrison held her hand in his, and they watched the stars flicker above them.

She leaned against his shoulder, feeling his warmth and enjoying his company. She'd gotten so used to being around him but knew that he and his mother would be returning to Chicago soon.

Timing was everything in life, sometimes. And she and Harrison had met at a time when their lives were in different cities.

He turned to her and tilted her chin up, one hand stroking her face. "Nora, I have something to say to you. My grandfather encouraged me to say it, actually."

"Your grandfather?"

"Never let things go unsaid to someone you love."

Her heart skipped a beat.

"And I love you, Nora Cassidy. Probably from the first moment I met you. It just took me a while to figure it out."

"But we're from different worlds," she protested.

"Everything can be overcome if we try."

"But my life is here. I can't give up the lodge, and your job is in Chicago." She knew her protests about geography weren't the real problem. She *knew* that.

"Nora, we can work things out. Tell me you want to try." His eyes held a determination in them, imploring her to just… try.

But she couldn't say yes. Not yet.

"I… I need some time."

His forehead creased. "You care about me too, don't you?"

"Harrison, really, I need some time to… think."

He nodded then because he was quintessentially a gentleman after all.

Her emotions rolled, and her thoughts ricocheted like a snowball barreling down a mountain.

She looked at him in the moonlight and knew without a doubt that she cared about him. And that scared her. She didn't know if it was enough to overcome...

She looked out at the lake.

To overcome her guilt and the feeling that she would be leaving Ronnie behind.

CHAPTER 31

She sat beside the lake on her favorite rock the next evening. Ronnie had been noticeably absent these last few days. "Ronnie, I need you. I need to talk to you. I need to figure out what to do."

She could understand exactly how Harrison's grandfather had felt when he'd gotten close to Linda's mother. And the guilt he'd felt even though his wife was gone. So Vernon had pushed Patricia away because of his guilt. And look what a mess had come from that.

She turned at the sound of a noise beside the lake. "Ronnie," she whispered.

The blue heron walked right up to within a couple of yards of her.

"Ronnie, I need a sign. Something to tell me what to do." She knew she was ridiculous talking to a bird, but... still...

The heron looked at her, and she swore he bobbed his head in a yes. He looked at her one more time and then stretched his majestic wings, took a few wobbly steps, and flew off over the lake.

She looked up at the heavens. "I'll always love you, Ronnie. Nothing will ever change that."

The heron circled back around and flew over her head, dipping once in his flight until he disappeared into the distance.

She looked down at her left hand, staring at the silver wedding band that had been on her finger for so many years. She slowly slipped it off her finger and carefully placed it in her pocket.

At that very moment, snow began to gently fall around her. She lifted her face and let the flakes slowly drift onto her skin, melting as they rolled down her cheeks. Soon, they mingled with her tears.

"Thank you, Ronnie," she whispered.

The snow began covering the ground in a

beautiful new blanket of white. Everything looked fresh and new. A new beginning.

"It's going to be okay, isn't it?" she whispered to the wind gently tossing the snow across the ground. "It's okay to move on and find happiness."

She lifted her face to the falling flakes of snow. The first snowfall of the year had always been her thing. She looked forward to it every year. And every single year since she'd been a little girl, she'd gone out and thrown herself into the snow and made a snow angel.

That is until the year that Ronnie died. It had seemed... frivolous... to abandon everything and throw herself into the snow. It was just a young girl thing she'd done. Then she'd become a single parent without time for just... fun.

She watched while the snow began to gather, covering the ground. The storm gathered in intensity, dumping the white fluffy flakes all around her.

Without thinking it through, without stopping to think about how *ridiculous* it was... she scampered off the rock and threw herself down in the pristine white patch of snow beside the lake.

She flung out her arms wide and scooted her legs back and forth.

A snow angel.

A smile crept across her face. The first snowfall. Her snow angel had returned.

She sensed more than heard the approach of footsteps, and she knew it would be Harrison. Knew it. Felt it deep inside her. She turned her head.

He stood there watching her. "Snow angel?"

"Yep. Always the right thing to do on the first snowfall of the year."

"Well, then, who am I to argue with tradition?" He dropped to the snow beside her, flung out his arms and legs, and scraped an angel into the snow. He left his arm outstretched, inches from hers.

She reached out farther and tangled her fingers in his. And just like Harrison's grandfather had told him to never let words go unsaid with someone you love—because she *did* love Harrison, she knew it in that very moment—she turned her face to look at him.

His clear blue eyes were staring at her.

"Harrison, there's something you should know."

"What's that?" His voice was low and hushed in the falling snow.

"It appears I've fallen in love with you."

"You have?" A wide grin spread across his face.

Everything felt exactly right at that moment. She'd never been so certain of anything in her life. "I have. Definitely."

"So, what are we going to do about that?"

"I'm thinking you should kiss me."

Harrison stood and reached out a hand to help her to her feet.

"Then, I guess I should kiss you. If you insist." He leaned down and kissed her while the snow drifted down around them in a perfect blanket of peacefulness.

He finally pulled away, and they turned to look at the snow angels they'd carved into the first snowfall.

He held her hand tightly in his, connecting with her, filling her with a contentment and peace that flowed through her. "Nora, you know what I'd like?"

"What?"

"I'd like to be here to make snow angels with you at the first snowfall of every year."

"I'd like that too."

And they sealed their hopes and dreams with another kiss.

CHAPTER 32

Annie stood at Nora's side, one arm gently wrapped around her shoulder. "Oh, Nora, you look beautiful."

Nora looked in the mirror at the simple dress she'd chosen for her wedding—with Annie's help, of course.

"Are you nervous?" Annie smoothed an imaginary wrinkle from the dress.

"A little bit. I've been single for a lot of years." So many years. She and Harrison had hired Zach Berry to build them a new cabin on the property. Although she was sad to think of leaving the cabin she'd lived in for all so long, it was time for a change. A new beginning.

"Looks like we'll both be old married women now."

Nora was so grateful to have her friend by her side, as always. Traveling through life, no matter what changed, no matter what life threw at them, they were always there for each other. She gave Annie a tight hug.

"What's that for?" Annie's mouth turned up in a smile.

"For being my best friend. For being here with me when I need you."

"Always."

Beth came hurrying into the room. She paused and stared at Nora. "Oh, Mom, you look beautiful."

"That's what *I* said." Annie nodded.

"Oh, quit it, you two. You're just used to seeing me in jeans and t-shirts." She turned and took another look in the mirror. It was easy to see the years on her face, even with the touch of makeup Annie had helped her carefully apply. But she was fine with the few wrinkles and scattered gray hairs. She'd earned them. Each and every one of them. And none of them had scared Harrison away.

She smiled. Harrison. She was marrying Harrison. Today. Right now. Okay, maybe she *was* nervous.

"I'm just so happy for you." Beth handed

her a simple bouquet of flowers. "Cece said we're ready to start whenever you are."

"I'm ready." She was. She couldn't wait to walk down the aisle of the chalet and become Harrison's wife.

Cece poked her head into the room. "All set?"

Nora nodded. A few moments later, the music started and Beth opened the door. She watched while Beth and then Annie walked down the aisle. Annie looked back and smiled at her.

She stood in the doorway. Her turn.

She *was* all set. Wasn't she?

All of a sudden, a rush of nervousness surged through her. This was going to change her whole life. Everything familiar had been turned upside down. She paused in the doorway, sucking in deep breaths.

Then she saw him. Harrison. Standing at the end of the aisle, a wide just-for-her smile on his face. He held out a hand toward her as if he knew she needed his support.

And just like that, the nervousness faded, and she took a confident step down the aisle to Harrison, the man who she loved. The man who loved her—and she was certain of that.

She wanted to share each and every day of the rest of her life with him. Her heart beat in a syncopated rhythm of happiness and joy as she walked down the aisle and placed her hand in Harrison's.

~

DEAR READER,

I hope you enjoy the Sweet River series. I loved writing all these characters. If you enjoyed this series, be sure and check out my other books. Information on all my books can be found my website.

Or jump right in and try the first book in my Lighthouse Point series.

Wish Upon a Shell - Book One

Or try the Comfort Crossing series:

The Shop on Main - Book One

As always, I appreciate each and every one of you. Happy reading!

Kay

THANK YOU for reading my story. I hope you enjoyed it. Sign up for my newsletter to be updated with information on new releases, promotions, give-aways, and newsletter-only surprises. The signup is at my website, kaycorrell.com.

Reviews help other readers find new books. I always appreciate when my readers take time to leave an honest review.

I love to hear from my readers. Feel free to contact me at authorcontact@kaycorrell.com

COMFORT CROSSING ~ THE SERIES

The Shop on Main - Book One

The Memory Box - Book Two

The Christmas Cottage - A Holiday Novella (Book 2.5)

The Letter - Book Three

The Christmas Scarf - A Holiday Novella (Book 3.5)

The Magnolia Cafe - Book Four

The Unexpected Wedding - Book Five

The Wedding in the Grove (crossover short story between the Comfort Crossing and Lighthouse Point series - Josephine and Paul from The Letter.)

LIGHTHOUSE POINT ~ THE SERIES

Wish Upon a Shell - Book One

Wedding on the Beach - Book Two

Love at the Lighthouse - Book Three

Cottage near the Point - Book Four

Return to the Island - Book Five

Bungalow by the Bay - Book Six

SWEET RIVER ~ THE SERIES

A Dream to Believe in - Book One

A Memory to Cherish - Book Two

A Song to Remember - Book Three

A Time to Forgive - Book Four

A Summer of Secrets - Book Five

A Moment in the Moonlight - Book Six

INDIGO BAY ~ Save by getting Kay's complete collection of stories previously published separately in the multi-author Indigo Bay series. The three stories are all interconnected.

Sweet Days by the Bay

Or buy them separately:

Sweet Sunrise - Book Three

Sweet Holiday Memories - a short holiday story

Sweet Starlight - Book Nine

ABOUT THE AUTHOR

Kay writes sweet, heartwarming stories that are a cross between women's fiction and contemporary romance. She is known for her charming small towns, quirky townsfolk, and enduring strong friendships between the women in her books.

Kay lives in the Midwest of the U.S. and can often be found out and about with her camera, taking a myriad of photographs which she likes to incorporate into her book covers. When not lost in her writing or photography, she can be found spending time with her ever-supportive husband, knitting, or playing with her puppies —two cavaliers and one naughty but adorable Australian shepherd. Kay and her husband also love to travel. When it comes to vacation time, she is torn between a nice trip to the beach or the mountains—but the mountains only get considered in the summer—she swears she's allergic to snow.

Learn more about Kay and her books at kaycorrell.com

While you're there, sign up for her newsletter to hear about new releases, sales, and giveaways.

WHERE TO FIND ME:
kaycorrell.com
authorcontact@kaycorrell.com

Join my Facebook Reader Group. We have lots of fun and you'll hear about sales and new releases first!
https://www.facebook.com/groups/KayCorrell/

f facebook.com/KayCorrellAuthor

instagram.com/kaycorrell

pinterest.com/kaycorrellauthor

amazon.com/author/kaycorrell

BB bookbub.com/authors/kay-correll